P9-DGF-231

BOOKS BY

JUNICHIRŌ TANIZAKI

Some Prefer Nettles (1955)

The Makioka Sisters (1957)

The Key (1963)

Seven Japanese Tales (1963)

Diary of a Mad Old Man (1965)

*These are Borzoi Books
published in New York by
Alfred A. Knopf*

❀❀❀❀❀

The Secret History
of the Lord of Musashi

AND

Arrowroot

JUNICHIRŌ TANIZAKI

The Secret History
of the Lord of Musashi

AND

Arrowroot

TRANSLATED BY
ANTHONY H. CHAMBERS

Alfred A. Knopf   New York   1982

THIS IS A BORZOI BOOK
PUBLISHED BY ALFRED A. KNOPF, INC.

Translation Copyright © 1982 by Alfred A. Knopf, Inc.

All rights reserved under International and Pan-American
Copyright Conventions. Published in the United States by
Alfred A. Knopf, Inc., New York, and simultaneously in
Canada by Random House of Canada Limited, Toronto.
Distributed by Random House, Inc., New York.

*Bushūkō Hiwa (The Secret History of the Lord of
Musashi)*, serialized in *Shinseinen* in 1931–32, was revised
by the author and published by Chūō Kōronsha in 1935.
Yoshino Kuzu (Arrowroot) was first published in the
January and February 1931 issues of *Chūō Kōron*. In 1932
it was included in a volume with *A Blind Man's Tale*
and two folktales. Some of the paper used for the 1932
edition was made in Kuzu, and the calligraphy was done
by Matsuko Nezu, soon to be Tanizaki's wife.

Library of Congress Cataloging in Publication Data
Tanizaki, Jun'ichirō, 1886–1965.
The secret history of the Lord of Musashi;
and, Arrowroot.
Translation of: Bushō Kō hiwa and Yoshino-kuzu.
I. Tanizaki, Jun'ichirō, 1886–1965.
Yoshino-kuzu. English. 1982. II. Title.
PL839.A7A23   1982   895.6'34   81-48257
ISBN 0-394-52454-3   AACR2

Manufactured in the United States of America
FIRST EDITION

Contents

Introduction

❧❧ ❧❧ ❧❧ ❧❧ ❧❧

In 1948, after completing his great novel *The Makioka Sisters*, Tanizaki wrote that of his works he actually liked *Some Prefer Nettles* (1928–29) and *Arrowroot* (1930) best. *The Secret History of the Lord of Musashi*, written in 1931–32, was another favorite. He often spoke of writing a sequel, a sketchy outline for which was found after his death.

Arrowroot and *The Secret History of the Lord of Musashi* are from the middle years of Tanizaki's extraordinary career. By the time he wrote *Arrowroot*, the novels, stories, plays, and essays of his first twenty years of writing had already been collected and published as his *Complete Works*, but he was to go on shocking and entertaining his readers with new works and adding to his distinctions for another thirty-five years. In 1949 he received the Imperial Award for Cultural Merit, and in 1964 was elected to honorary membership in the American Academy and Institute of Arts and Letters, the first Japanese writer to be so honored.

The two pieces included in this volume show the extremes of Tanizaki's versatility. Yet they share the fundamental characteristics of all of his fiction: the pursuit of the Ideal Woman; an awareness that, as Wordsworth said, "the Child is father of the Man"; a rich, eloquent style; and, above all, the old-fashioned pleasure of a good story brilliantly told.

From 1910 until about 1930, Tanizaki preferred an "orthodox" novelistic style, "propelled by strictly objective description and dialogue," as in *Some Prefer Nettles*. But from 1930 to 1935 he experimented with a subtler, more subjective "essay-fiction," the object of which was to "find the form that would convey the greatest feeling of reality." At the same time, a renewed interest in Japanese history and aesthetics is apparent in his writings from about 1926 on. In *Arrowroot* he brought his new interests, experimentation and tradition, together for the first time. Having arrived at this happy combination, he exploited it in a series of masterworks, including *A Blind Man's Tale* (1931), *The Secret History of the Lord of Musashi, Ashikari* (1932), *A Portrait of Shunkin* (1933), and *The Mother of Captain Shigemoto* (1949).

The narrative technique of both *Arrowroot* and *The Secret History* seems to have been inspired by Stendhal's *The Abbess of Castro*, which Tanizaki translated into Japanese in 1928. The narrator of Stendhal's story, much like the narrator of *Arrowroot*, travels to a remote part of Italy to search out the truth of a story that has been covered up by partisan historians, and, like the narrator of *The Secret History*, he bases his story on two old manuscripts. There is a difference, however: Stendhal used real Italian manuscripts as the basis for the tales in *Chroniques Italiennes*, of which *The Abbess of Castro* is one; but Tanizaki fabricated the manuscripts on which *The Secret History* purports to be based, and all the characters and events (except for several warlords mentioned in the Preface and in Book I) are fictional. The sources mentioned in *Arrowroot*, on the other hand, are all authentic.

The reader should not assume, by the way, that the narrator of *Arrowroot* is Tanizaki himself. "The 'mother' that is mentioned in this work is the mother of Tsumura's friend, not my mother," the author wrote in 1964. "My mother was born in Fukagawa, Edo, in 1864, and died in

Kakigara-chō, Nihombashi, Tokyo, in 1917. A pure child of Tokyo, she never set foot in Western Japan."

Indeed, Tanizaki's fiction is far less autobiographical than that of most Japanese novelists. He preferred to use his imagination. "I have acquired a bad habit recently," he wrote in 1926.

> I cannot bring myself to write or read anything that takes real facts for its material, or that is even realistic. This is one reason that I make no attempt to read the works of contemporary authors that appear in the magazines every month. I'll scan the first five or six lines, say to myself, "Aha! he's writing about himself," and lose all desire to go on reading. Generally I read things that have nothing to do with the present. When I read historical novels, non-sense tales, even realistic novels of fifty years ago, or contemporary Western novels far removed from Japanese society, I can enjoy them as so many imaginary worlds.

As one might expect, then, it was the magical aura surrounding the legends of Yoshino that drew Tanizaki there and inspired him to write *Arrowroot*. In 1964 he recalled:

> Cherry-blossom viewing in Tokyo is simply a matter of sitting in a tea room behind bamboo screens, eating dumplings, roast taro and hard-boiled eggs, and drinking bottled Masamune. In the shadow of these flowers are no Yoshi-tsune, Wakaba-no-Naishi, Shizuka, Tadanobu, or Genkurō the fox, no Hatsune drum or Hiodoshi armor. Blossom viewing without these associations did not seem to me like blossom viewing at all. . . . There is no fantasy in the Tokyo blossoms. But when I went to see the famous blossom sites in Western Japan, I felt as though I might somewhere meet the phantom of Wakaba-no-Naishi or Lady Shizuka, and at times I even felt as if I had turned into a fox or into Gonta and was wandering about, lured by the sound of a drum or a whistle.

Like the narrator of *Arrowroot*, Tanizaki may originally have planned to write, as he suggested in 1933, a long historical novel along the lines of *Quo Vadis?*, set in medieval Japan, with courtiers, shōgun, priests, and beautiful women involved in deep, complex relationships and undergoing vast changes. *The Secret History of the Lord of Musashi* is the partial fruit of this ambition. Tanizaki found the traditional Japanese histories, which were strongly influenced by Confucian orthodoxy, to be drab and excessively didactic, and he deplored the Confucian influence on Japanese letters:

> We will never know how many geniuses were lost to so-called light literature thanks to the notion, current during the feudal period, that novels and the theater were for the diversion of women and children and were not suitable entertainment for samurai. A man of letters like Rai Sanyō [1780–1832], for example, would probably have written political or historical novels with some human warmth instead of that stiff *Unofficial History of Japan.*

The traditional Confucian and Buddhist attitude toward women—that they are inferior creatures, scarcely worthy of serious attention—was also reflected in historical records, to Tanizaki's distress. In 1931 he wrote:

> I frequently think that I would like to write a historical novel based on some person of the past, but I am always frustrated by the difficulty of forming a clear picture of the women who surrounded him. . . . Since ancient times Japanese family genealogies, from that of the Imperial Family down, have given comparatively detailed accounts of the activities of men, but when a woman appears she is simply noted as "woman" or "female," usually with no indication of the year of her birth or death, or even of her name. In other words, there are individual men in our history, but there is no such thing as an individual woman.

The following year he wrote:

My wish has been to re-create the psychology of Japanese women of the feudal period just as it was, without imposing modern interpretations, and to portray it in a way that will appeal to the emotions and understanding of modern readers. . . . Even a woman who appeared to be chaste and pure no doubt felt an immoral love, unperceived by others; jealousy, hatred, cruelty, and other depraved passions must have passed faintly through her heart. But it is extremely difficult to portray convincingly a woman who never gave the slightest outward sign of these feelings, whose entire life was lived inside herself.

This was written just before *The Secret History of the Lord of Musashi* and the creation of the passionate, tormented Lady Kikyō.

As it supplements the staid Confucian histories, *The Secret History* also burlesques them. The same aspects of life that the Confucian historians piously omitted from their accounts, Tanizaki presents in outrageous exaggeration. The narrator never questions the veracity of the preposterous events he has uncovered, though he questions the motivations of the Lord of Musashi's biographers and speculates cautiously on the lord's psychology. At the same time, he seems to be parodying his own sadomasochistic writings, as he does in *Diary of a Mad Old Man*. This ability to laugh at himself publicly is one of Tanizaki's most attractive qualities.

The translations are based on the texts in *Tanizaki Jun'-ichirō Zenshū* (28 volumes; Chūō Kōronsha, 1966–68). I am indebted to Hashimoto Yoshiichirō's annotations to *Arrowroot* in *Tanizaki Jun'ichirō Shū, Nihon Kindai Bungaku Taikei*, vol. 30 (Kadokawa Shoten, 1971). Many people have helped at various stages of the translations. I should like to thank Robert Campbell, Andrea F. Chambers, and Yoshiko Yokochi Samuel, who read the first draft of the translations and made a great many valuable suggestions. Some of the work has been done with the support of the Mansfield Freeman Fund of Wesleyan University. The translations, as were the original stories, are gratefully dedicated to Mrs. Matsuko Tanizaki.

ANTHONY H. CHAMBERS

The Secret History
of the Lord of Musashi

Preface

✖✖✖✖✖

It is said that the warlord Uesugi Kenshin loved his young pages. It is said, too, that Fukushima Masanori followed in the way of the Han Emperor Ai, who cut off the sleeve of his robe rather than waken the boy at his side. Masanori's proclivities grew more pronounced with age and finally led to his downfall. Nor are Kenshin and Masanori isolated examples. Many strange tales could be told about the sexual lives of men known to history as valiant heroes. Their habits, including pederasty and sadism, arose from the warrior's way of life and are not for us to censure too harshly.

This volume tells the story of the Lord of Musashi, born in the sixteenth-century Period of Civil Wars and known everywhere for his cunning and strength. He was the boldest, cruelest leader of his age. But those close to him said that he had masochistic sexual desires. Could this be true? I did not know whether to believe the extraordinary rumors, but he was a man to be pitied if they were true. His sexual tendencies are not mentioned in the official histories, and most people know nothing of them. But I recently examined some secret documents in the possession of the Kiryū family and learned what sort of man he really was. I felt the greatest sympathy for him when I found that he held an obsessive passion for a beautiful, refined woman. As Wang Yang-ming said, it is easier to subdue a bandit in the mountains than to subdue the evil in your heart. Yet the Lord of Musashi had the courage of a roaring tiger, and few in history could equal his ability to bring peace to the land. Deeply moved by his story, I decided to recount the details of his sexual life in the form of a historical novel. I have called it *The Secret History of the Lord of Musashi.* I pray you will not rashly dismiss it as an absurd fabrication.

Early autumn, 1935   THE AUTHOR

Contents

✿✿✿✿✿

Contents

Book I

✿ ✿ ✿ ✿ ✿

Concerning the Nun Myōkaku's "The Dream
of a Night" and the Memoirs of Dōami

There is no way of knowing exactly who the nun Myōkaku
was or when she wrote "The Dream of a Night," but it is
clear from the text that she was once in the service of the
Lord of Musashi. After the fall of the lord's clan, she shaved
her head and retired "to a thatched hut deep in the mountains, where there was nothing to do but pray to the
Buddha day and night." Thus it would seem that she recorded her memoirs of the past in the idleness of old age.
But why would a nun with "nothing to do but pray to the
Buddha" want to compose such a memoir? She gives this
explanation:

> After pondering the conduct of the Lord of Musashi, I
> understand that men are neither good nor evil, heroic nor
> timid. The grand are sometimes base and the brave some-
> times weak; he who yesterday crushed a thousand foes on
> the battlefield is lashed today at home by the fiends of hell.
> The most graceful woman may show a ferocious temper;
> the most valiant warrior may suddenly turn into a beast.
> Perhaps the Lord of Musashi was a compassionate Buddha
> or Bodhisattva who, demonstrating in his own person the
> inexorable law of cause and effect and the cycle of trans-
> migration, appeared in this world for a time to lead us out
> of illusion.

She concludes that

by enduring the torments of hell in his own precious body, the Lord of Musashi showed us common mortals the way to enlightenment. His presence was a blessing to us all. I am writing this account of his activities out of gratitude for his kindness and as an offering for the repose of his soul. I have no other purpose. If there be those who laugh in scorn at the lord's behavior, they shall be the damned. People of understanding will feel only gratitude.

Her argument seems a bit strained, however, and there is reason to wonder whether she really believed her own explanation. She lived alone, of course, and thus her biological needs were not satisfied; perhaps she wrote in an attempt to ease her desolation. But this is only idle speculation.

The author of "Confessions of Dōami" gives no indication of his motives, but it is obvious that he could not erase from his memory either "my lord's terrifying behavior" or his own extraordinary experiences in the service of his master. No doubt these adventures seemed stranger to him the more he thought about them and, in the end, the temptation to put everything down in writing was irresistible. While the nun Myōkaku arrived at the happy but unlikely conclusion that the Lord of Musashi was a Bodhisattva incarnate, Dōami appears to have had a clear understanding of his master's mentality and to have earned his confidence as a result. From time to time the lord would reveal his inner anguish to Dōami and relate the history of his sexual appetites out of a need for sympathy and understanding. Dōami, for his part, seems to have been something of a sycophant. Perhaps he shared the lord's proclivities by nature; if not, he feigned them to curry favor and in the process became a true convert. In any case, it is certain that Dōami was an indispensable companion in the lord's "secret paradise." Without Dōami the lord's sex games probably would not have taken their perverse course, and, for this very reason, he sometimes cursed Dōami's existence. He often beat him and more than once came close to dispatching him with his sword. But Dōami was singularly fortunate: few of the men and women who participated in the lord's "games" escaped with their lives. Being the most vulnerable, Dōami must have faced death more often than anyone else. No doubt he escaped the tiger's jaws because he was prized as much as he was hated, but in part survival was his reward for alertness and tact.

Concerning the Armor of Terukatsu, Lord of Musashi, and the Portrait of Lady Shōsetsuin

A portrait now in the possession of the descendants of the Kiryū clan shows Terukatsu sitting cross-legged on a tiger skin, fully clad in armor with a European breastplate, black-braided shoulder plates, taces and fur boots. His helmet is surmounted by enormous, sweeping horns, like a water buffalo's. He holds a tasseled baton of command in his right hand; his left hand is spread so wide on his thigh that the thumb reaches the scabbard of his sword. If he were not wearing armor, one could get some idea of his physique; dressed as he is, only the face is visible. It is not uncommon to see likenesses of heroes from the Period of Civil Wars clad in full armor, and Terukatsu's portrait is very similar to those of Honda Heihachirō and Sakakibara Yasumasa that so often appear in history books. They all give an impression of great dignity and severity, but at the same time there is an uncomfortable stiffness and formality in the way they square their shoulders.

Historical sources indicate that Terukatsu died at the age of forty-two. He looks somewhat younger than that in this portrait, perhaps between thirty-five and forty. With his full cheeks and strong, square jaw, he is certainly not an ugly man, though his eyes, nose, and mouth are disproportionately large. All in all, it is a face worthy of an intelligent and self-assured leader. His eyes, open wide and glaring straight ahead, glitter angrily from under the peak of his helmet. Between the eyes and above the nose is a slight bulging of the flesh, cut horizontally by a deep crease so that it looks almost like a second, very small nose. Deep wrinkles run from either side of his nose to the corners of his mouth, giving him an irritable look, as if he had just chewed something bitter. He has a straggly mustache and goatee, in the fashion of the times.

Impressive as this face is, it would be far less imposing without the helmet. In addition to the splendid horns, there is a crest on the brow of the helmet depicting Taishakuten, the Buddhist guardian of the east, crushing a demon underfoot. The European breastplate, too, is strangely impressive. I am no authority on the subject, but it seems that the Western-style breastplate was introduced to Japan by the Dutch or Portuguese in the 1530s or '40s, about the time matchlocks first came in through Tanegashima. It might be described as pigeon-breast armor: like a peach, it swells to a ridge down the center, and the bottom edge curves up and away toward the back. The warlords of the period set a high value on such breastplates—so much so that imitations were being manufactured not long after their introduction —and so it is perhaps not remarkable that Terukatsu should be wearing one. Still, why did he choose this particular armor for his portrait? We do not know whether he commissioned the portrait himself or someone painted it from memory after his death; but in either case the portrait is evidence, I think, that this European breastplate was Terukatsu's favorite piece of armor.

If one views the portrait knowing the Lord of Musashi

only as he is presented in the history books, then it will seem no more than the portrait of a hero, resembling those of Honda Tadakatsu and Sakakibara Yasumasa. But one who knows about the lord's weaknesses and has learned the secrets of his sexual life will detect (or is it just the power of suggestion?) a certain anxiety behind the imposing façade—the anguish of the lord's soul concealed within forbidding armor—and the image will seem pervaded with an unspeakable melancholy. The glaring eyes, for example, the tight lips, the angry nose, and the set of the shoulders would inspire the same awe in a viewer as the picture of a bloodthirsty tiger; and yet, seen in a different frame of mind, Terukatsu looks like a man suffering from rheumatism and struggling to endure the excruciating pain in his joints. The European breastplate and the helmet, with its sweeping horns and Taishakuten crest, are open to suspicion as well. Perhaps he chose these formidable trappings deliberately to conceal his inner weakness. But the effect of these accessories is to make the rigidly posing figure seem all the more awkward and artificial. The pigeon-breast armor would look less uncomfortable if Terukatsu were perched on a stool in the Western style, but because he is sitting cross-legged, the breastplate juts forward ungracefully. There is no suggestion of the muscular, battle-hard flesh that must have been there behind the plate. The armor does not cling to his body as it should and seems somehow independent. Far from protecting his person and instilling awe in others, it looks like a set of shackles inflicting endless torture on him. When viewed in this light, the lord's countenance betrays a touching look of anguish, and the figure of the brave, armor-clad warrior comes to resemble a prisoner moaning grimly in the stocks. If the decoration on the front of the helmet is viewed with a skeptical eye, the figure of Taishakuten standing triumphantly over a demon symbolizes the lord's courage, while the hideous, grimacing demon itself, trampled cruelly underfoot, hints at the shameful side of the lord's character. Of course the artist, as he worked, had no such intent. Probably he knew nothing of the lord's secret life and simply painted an objective likeness.

On a matching scroll stored in the same box is a portrait of the lord's wife. Neither is signed, but it is safe to assume that the two likenesses were executed by the same artist at about the same time. The lady was a daughter of Chirifu, Lord of Shinano, a daimyo of about the same standing as the Kiryū clan. Noted for her faithful service to her husband Terukatsu, she took the tonsure after his death and assumed the religious name of Shōsetsuin. She was supported by her father's family, but her last years were particularly lonely, as she had no children. She survived her husband by only three years.

It is characteristic of portraits of historical figures in Japan that many of the paintings of men are realistic masterpieces with individual traits carefully rendered, but those of women are nothing more than stereotyped representations of whatever the age considered to be the ideal model of beauty. The lady in this portrait has fine, regular features and is beautiful, to be sure, but the painting is not much different from those of other daimyo wives of the same period. It could just as well be a portrait of the wife of Hosokawa Tadaoki or Bessho Nagaharu; the impression made on the viewer would be virtually the same.

Typically there is an icy detachment in the blanched faces of these stereotyped beauties, and this lady is no exception. Her face is round and full, but on close inspection the pasty white makeup appears to be flaking here and there, and her cheeks are quite lifeless. The same is true of her proud, sculpturesque nose. Above all, her eyes—long, narrow slits with the pupils gleaming like needles under stately lids—give an impression of coldness as well as refined intelligence. No doubt the wives of daimyo in that period spent their monotonous days shut up in the inner suites of their palaces, where light rarely penetrated, and so perhaps they all assumed this characteristic expression. The loneliness, boredom, and despair that Terukatsu's wife suffered were particularly severe, and one senses that this portrait must indeed show her true countenance.

Book II

✳ ✳ ✳ ✳ ✳

In Which Hōshimaru Grows Up as a Hostage in Ojika Castle, and Concerning Woman-Heads

"Confessions of Dōami" contains this account:

> My lord's childhood name was Hōshimaru. He was the eldest son and heir of Terukuni, Lord of Musashi; but when he was six years old he was sent as a hostage to the castle on Mount Ojika, the seat of the lord Tsukuma Ikkansai of the next province, with whom his father had reached a reconciliation. My lord told me, "I was separated from my father at an early age. For more than ten years I studied the literary and military arts at the castle on Mount Ojika. I am indebted to Ikkansai for my upbringing."

This passage mentions a "reconciliation," but the head of the Tsukuma clan was a major daimyo with several provinces under his rule, and so Terukuni was certainly not an equal partner in the "reconciliation," though he may have been spared the humiliation of a complete surrender. It is likely that he became Ikkansai's vassal, for he would not otherwise have offered his son and heir as hostage.

What follows is one of the few surviving episodes from Hōshimaru's early years.

In the autumn of 1549, when Hōshimaru was twelve years old, the castle on Mount Ojika was besieged for more than a month by the forces of Yakushiji Danjō Masataka, a vassal of the Hatakeyama family, who were, in turn, hereditary officials in the shogunate. Hōshimaru had not yet come of age and so was not permitted to join the fighting, but the daily battle reports he heard inside the castle made his young heart pound. He realized that a boy his age could not go to war, but he was, after all, the son of a samurai family. At the very least he wanted to view the battle for himself. Though he was too young for his first campaign, he reasoned it was none too soon to slip out onto the battlefield and learn how a warrior conducts himself. But the castle on Mount Ojika—the headquarters of the Tsukuma clan for generations—was a heavily guarded labyrinth. It would have been impossible to slip outside unnoticed. The hostages were watched closely after the siege began, and Hōshimaru was personally attended by a samurai who had come with him from his father's castle. Hōshimaru found him useful in many ways, but he could also be meddlesome. Shut up all day in the room assigned to him, Hōshimaru would listen to the distant gunfire and battle cries as Aoki Shuzen, his attendant, described the progress of the battle. "That is the sound of the enemy being driven back," Shuzen would say; or, "That was the sound of a trumpet shell, signaling our men to regroup within the gates." It would be a hard fight, he explained. The enemy had already taken the advance fortifications surrounding the main castle, and more than twenty thousand soldiers encircled the base of Mount Ojika. There were fewer than five thousand defenders. Thanks to strong fortifications and a strategic position, the castle had been able to hold out so far, but time was on the side of the attackers, and nearly a month had passed. The only hope was that political changes in Kyoto might lead the enemy to raise their siege; if this did not occur soon, the castle would fall.

Technically, Hōshimaru was a hostage, but undoubtedly he was accorded special treatment as the son of a daimyo and was given a comfortable room in the keep. But gradually the spacious castle shrank. The attackers took the outer works, then invaded the third citadel and drove its occupants into the second. As the second citadel filled up, people swarmed into the keep, crowding every room and turret. At the same time, the orderly assignment of posts began to slacken: each man had a designated battle station, but now anyone with a free hand helped out where he was needed. Even Aoki Shuzen could not always stay at his young master's side, following the desperate battle from a distance. When the attack was especially fierce, he would take up a position and join in the defense. Dōami quotes his master as saying,

"When I look back on my childhood, even events that were humiliating at the time have become precious memories. During the siege of Mount Ojika, I was forced to live with no-account women and children and could learn nothing about battle strategy. I was mortified; but, in retrospect, it was an interesting experience."

In short, Hōshimaru was delighted at the slackening of Aoki Shuzen's supervision. His room, which had been so isolated from the excitement of battle, grew lively as unfamiliar women and children crowded in. No doubt they were hostages, too, assembled in Hōshimaru's room to keep them out of the soldiers' way. Children seem to relish chaotic situations—wars, earthquakes, fires, and the like, when large numbers of people take refuge together and make a commotion—just as they would enjoy a camping trip. Hōshimaru may have been mortified to find himself thrown together with "no-account women and children," but as a highborn youth who had seen little of the world he must also have felt his curiosity awakened. In particular, his interest was aroused by a group of elderly matrons.

There were no mature men among the hostages, only young boys; but the women were of all ages, including grandmothers of fifty or sixty, middle-aged wives, and young girls. To Hōshimaru, they were "no-accounts," but since they were there as hostages they must have been women of high birth from good samurai houses. The best evidence of this is that they never lost their composure, even during the fiercest attacks, but waited calmly in their corner of the room, reserved and discreet. All of them— even the youngest—seemed to have experienced war before. They talked quietly together, just as they might chat over tea, appraising the course of the fighting from the sound of battle cries and the rumble of war drums. "There will probably be an attack tonight," they would say knowledgeably; or, "We can expect a surprise attack in the morning." Because he had no one to explain the battle to him now that Aoki Shuzen had become a participant, Hōshimaru began to eavesdrop on the women's conversations. He wanted to be included in their circle but was shy, as all of them were older than he, and so he would listen casually from a distance or loiter in their part of the room on one pretext or another. One evening, when the stronger women had returned from attending the wounded (there had been a violent engagement that day), they all began to talk over the day's events, and Hōshimaru moved quietly toward them.

"Hōshimaru!" An old woman in the group hailed him. "Hōshimaru, come join us." She gave him a reassuring look and smiled good-naturedly. Turning back to her companions, she said, "He is an admirable child. He pretends not to listen when we talk about the battle, but he is straining his ears. No doubt he will grow up to be a fine general." The old woman was of comparatively high rank and seemed to have the respect of all the others. She sat on a thick cushion, her elbow propped on an armrest, with about twenty women in a circle around her.

"Hōshimaru, do you want to hear about the fighting?" This time it was a different woman who spoke. Hōshimaru nodded. He felt the eyes of the entire group turn toward him as she spoke, and experienced an irrational terror— something like the panic one might feel if surrounded by some exotic tribe. The society of the time maintained a strict division between the sexes. What is more, the boy had been separated from his parents at an early age to be brought up among rough samurai, and so knew nothing of life in the fragrant, bewitching inner suites. The gathering of women before him was like a flower garden seen for the first time, sparkling with color and redolent of strange incense. He had been viewing them from a distance, but now as he drew close and was enveloped in their atmosphere, Hōshimaru was probably struck not by a sense of beauty or sensuality, but by an aversion to the unfamiliar. He stood silent for a time.

"Please, come sit here."

He nodded and sat down on the mat with a loud thump to hide his embarrassment.

"You will be able to go to battle in two or three years." One of the women had guessed what was on his mind.

"Yes, indeed. He's tall and sturdy; you can see at a glance that he has promise."

The women knew who Hōshimaru was and why he was there. No doubt they sympathized with his situation, as they, too, were hostages. Some of them probably had sons or younger brothers of about the same age.

"How I would like to see him in his first campaign," said one.

"The Lord of Musashi is fortunate to have such an heir."

None of this was of any interest to Hōshimaru. He wished they would hurry up and talk about the fighting. The old woman who had spoken first asked sympathetically, "Then you have never watched the enemy's movements?" The question was well-intentioned, but Hōshimaru took offense. His face flushed as he shook his head.

"I want to, but he won't let me. He says children can't go out to the second citadel."

His injured tone made the old woman smile. "Who said that to you?"

"The samurai attending me. He's always telling me I can't do this and I can't do that." Then Hōshimaru asked a question. "You have seen the attack from up close, haven't you?"

"Yes, when the fighting is brisk, as it was today, we do what we can to help. Sometimes we go up into the turrets, or even as far as the gate."

"Then you can watch them killing the enemy and taking their heads?"

"Oh, yes. Sometimes we get too close and are splashed with blood."

Hōshimaru looked up at the old woman's face with envy: grown-ups were so lucky, he thought, for even a woman could see all that. He could hardly contain himself.

"Take me with you tomorrow, will you?"

"Oh dear," said the old woman, still smiling fondly. "What a pity. We really could not do that. If we did, we should be scolded by Aoki Shuzen."

"Shuzen won't find out. And I won't get in your way. I can do anything you can."

"But a young gentleman like you simply does not help with women's work. People will laugh at you."

Hōshimaru had to agree with what the old woman said. But if he could not actually go to the field of battle, at least he wanted to see the body, even the head, of a famous warrior. The truth is, he had never seen a mutilated corpse or a raw, dripping head. He did remember having come across

a head on display somewhere, but he had never seen anything that evoked the glory of the battlefield. Of course it
is only natural that this should have been so. Brought up in
a samurai house, he was subject to the strictest supervision.
Even so, Hōshimaru was ashamed that he, the twelve-year-
old son of a general, should be so inexperienced. And at
such a time! Piles of dead soldiers were rising every day not
far from his room and even the women were so close to
the fighting that they were showered with blood. Only he
was lacking in experience. Nothing could be more humiliating. He wanted to test his courage, not because he
thought the sight of battle would frighten him, but because
he wanted to train himself now so that he would not be
caught off guard in his first campaign.

Such was the appeal Hōshimaru made to the old woman
two or three days later.

She thought for a moment. "All right, then," she said.
"I cannot take you to the battlefield, but if you want to see
some heads, I can arrange it for you. You must never tell
anyone. Do you understand? If you promise me that, I will
show you tonight what you want to see." She explained in
a whisper that almost every night five or six of the women
had been selected to attend to the enemy heads taken in
battle. They would check the heads against a list, label
them, and wash off the bloodstains. The heads of common
soldiers were another matter; but those of noted warriors
were carefully cleaned and presented to the commander for
inspection. The women would dress the hair, touch up the
dye on the teeth, and even, on occasion, apply some light
cosmetic to make the heads presentable. In short, they did
their best to reproduce the features and the coloring of
living heads. "Dressing heads," as it was called, was considered women's work, and, there being a shortage of
women in the castle, some of the hostages had been ordered

to help. Because all of them were friends, the old woman could take Hōshimaru in secret to watch.

"Do you understand? If anyone finds out, we will be in trouble. You must follow me without saying a word and watch quietly. And you must not try to help with the heads or speak any more than necessary." The old woman searched Hōshimaru's eyes as she spoke. They were burning with curiosity. "All right then," she said. "I will come for you tonight. Pretend that you are asleep and wait for me."

The women and children who had invaded Hōshimaru's room slept in rows without regard to age or rank. Only Hōshimaru and Aoki Shuzen slept apart from the rest, behind a screen at the head of the room. Luckily, the spacious chamber had only one flickering lamp, and behind the screen it was quite dark. Even if he woke up in the night, Shuzen would probably not notice that Hōshimaru's bed was empty. And Shuzen, exhausted from his daytime exertions, had been falling instantly into a deep sleep punctuated by loud snoring. Nor was Shuzen the only one who slept soundly. With the exception of the soldiers who kept watch by turns, everyone slept like the dead. The more furious the noise and activity during the day, the more eerily quiet the nights would be. In the hushed darkness, Hōshimaru waited breathlessly under his quilts. Soon he heard the old woman's footsteps, then a tapping on the screen.

"Which way?" The boy crept around the foot of Shuzen's bed and slipped past the screen.

"This way." The old woman pointed to the door with her chin. As he walked behind her, Hōshimaru could hear the rhythmical swishing of her silk robes, like the lapping of waves on a quiet sea.

It was a cold night in the middle of the Tenth Month.

The old woman wore a long starched robe over a white kimono; hunching her narrow shoulders, she held the skirt up with both hands to keep it from brushing the sleeping figures and to check the rustling sound. She did not carry a lantern, but when they emerged from the room into a passageway, they could see watch fires burning here and there in the garden. The light reflected off the polished floorboards and shone red in the old woman's face when she turned to signal Hōshimaru with her eyes. Her breath was white as she spoke. She no longer looked like the refined, warmhearted matron that he was used to seeing by daylight. The deep shadows in her sunken flesh gave her the haggard look of a demon mask. She seemed unkempt and much older than she had by day. He had noticed before that some of her hair was gray; now, as a fire flared in the distance, the silver strands at her temple caught the light and glowed like wires. Hōshimaru suddenly recalled Aoki Shuzen's repeated admonitions: "A person of good birth does not go off with someone he does not know. You must always speak to me before you go out." It was a plot, then, and he was heading into a trap! But at once he was ashamed of these cowardly thoughts. It was the night light that made the old woman's face so unearthly, nothing more. Still, to imagine danger was a sign of cowardice. That moment of doubt was a blow to his pride.

"Please put these on." When they reached the end of the passageway, the old woman noiselessly slid open the door and stepped down into the garden. Taking a pair of straw sandals from the folds of her kimono, she placed them before Hōshimaru. Because of the bright watch fires, he had not noticed the moon before, but once outside he could see that it was full and clear. The whitewashed walls all around him caught the moonlight and reflected it brightly onto the ground. The old woman walked quickly through the alternating light and shadow, following the white, zigzagging walls. She came to a small, two-story building, opened the door, and beckoned to Hōshimaru.

"This is the place."

Hōshimaru remembered the building. Weapons and armor had been stored in it, and there was a cramped upper floor, hardly more than an attic. When he followed the old woman inside, he saw that the interior had changed during the siege. All of the weapons and trunks had been removed for use in battle, leaving the room nearly empty. A makeshift stove had been constructed in one corner. Hōshimaru could make out this much by the light of the stove and by the penetrating moonlight. He also noticed an odd stench. The moldy smell peculiar to storehouses was partly responsible, but it was a complex odor, a blend of many things, and most unpleasant. And it was strangely warm and moist, perhaps because of the steam rising from a kettle of water on the stove.

"Here are the stairs. Please watch your step." The old woman led the way to the upper floor. Hōshimaru followed her and sat down in the bright lamplight at the top of the stairs.

Hōshimaru riveted his eyes on the most terrifying objects in the room, determined to let nothing frighten him. He looked first at the head placed before the woman nearest him, then, one by one, at the other heads set in a row. He was pleased to find that he could gaze calmly at any of them. In fact, the heads were so clean they did not look real, and they evoked none of the aura of battle or of the warrior's valor that Hōshimaru had expected. The longer he looked at them, the more artificial they seemed.

The women, apparently forewarned by the old woman, nodded politely to Hōshimaru as he entered the room and quietly went on with their work. Of the five women present, three sat with one head each before them, while the other two assisted. The first woman poured hot water into a basin and, with the help of one of the assistants, washed a head. When she was finished, she placed the head on a "head-board" and passed it to her neighbor. The second woman would dress the hair, and the third, attach a label. Finally, the head would be put in line with the other finished heads, on a long plank behind the women. So that they would not slide off, the heads were pressed firmly onto spikes that protruded from the surface of the plank.

The room was brightly lit by two lamps that had been placed among the women to illuminate their work, and the ceiling was so low that Hōshimaru would have struck a beam had he stood up. He could see everything in the room clearly. The heads themselves did not make a strong impression, but the contrast between the heads and the three women awakened a strange excitement in him. Compared to the pallor of the lifeless heads, the women's hands and fingers looked strangely vital, white, and voluptuous. The women grasped the heads by the topknot and, heads being quite heavy, twisted the hair around their wrists for a better grip. This seemed to enhance the strange beauty of their hands. Their faces were just as lovely. Used to their tasks, they worked mechanically and impassively, their faces as cold and unfeeling as stone. But somehow their impassivity was different from that of the heads. The one was hideous, the other sublime. And the women always treated the heads with respect, never roughly. Their movements were deliberate, modest, and graceful.

Hōshimaru was entranced. It was only later that he understood the emotion that had seized him; at the time, he forgot himself completely. It was an agitation that he had never experienced before, an inexpressible excitement. It occurred to him that the three women had been present that evening two or three days before when the old woman had first spoken to him. He remembered their faces, but he had felt nothing at the time. Why should they be so alluring now, face to face with heads in this attic? He watched each one as she performed her task. The woman at the far right attached a string to a wooden label and tied it to the topknot of the head before her. When a bald head—a "lay-priest head"—was passed to her, she poked a hole in one ear with an awl and passed the string through it. Hōshimaru felt an intense pleasure as he watched her make the hole. But he was most enraptured by the girl who sat in the middle, washing hair. She was the youngest of three—perhaps fifteen or sixteen. Her round face, though quite expressionless, had a natural charm. Now and then, as she gazed at a head, an unconscious smile would play about her lips. It was this smile that attracted Hōshimaru to her. At such moments, a guileless cruelty showed in her face. And her hands were more supple, more graceful as they dressed the hair, than the hands of the other women. From time to time she would take an incense burner from a table at her side and scent the hair. Then, when she had tied up the hair and adjusted the topknot, she would tap the crown of the head lightly with the back of her comb, in what appeared to be a gesture of courtesy. To Hōshimaru, she was irresistibly beautiful.

"Shall we go now?"

Hōshimaru blushed violently when the old woman spoke. She was the kindly, refined old woman once more, but as she looked at him, smiling pleasantly, he had the feeling that her eyes had penetrated his secret.

They had been in the room for no more than twenty or thirty minutes. Normally Hōshimaru would have asked the old woman to let him stay longer. It is only natural for a child to want to look at something unfamiliar, and it would not have been surprising had he demanded more time. But Hōshimaru had lost his youthful innocence. Prodded by the old woman, he reluctantly descended the stairs; but the enchantment lingered and kept him in a constant state of ecstasy.

At the entrance to the sleeping quarters, the old woman spoke again. "Have you seen enough? I planned this myself, and you must speak of it to no one." Her face was pressed close to his ear. "Do you understand? Then go back to bed quietly. Sleep well."

Hōshimaru was relieved to find Aoki Shuzen sleeping peacefully behind the screen; but once in bed, he could not calm his excitement and stared wide-eyed in the darkness. All through the night, phantoms floated up before him and vanished like foam on the sea—visions of heads strewn in the flickering light, their expressions, the color of their skin, their gory necks, voluptuous fingers working briskly among the silent shapes, and, above all, the lovely oval face of the young girl. He had witnessed an extraordinary scene. A dreadful stench had permeated everything; the women had been as silent as the severed heads. He had crept out of bed in the middle of the night and had been led through the pale, moonlit garden to that eerie place, and it had all ended so quickly. To a boy of twelve, it must have seemed that a separate, hidden world had unfolded before him for a moment, and then abruptly disappeared.

The enemy forces renewed their attack the next morning, and the smell of gunpowder, and the sounds of muskets, trumpet shells, war drums, and battle cries continued throughout the day. Again the hostage women faithfully did their part by carrying provisions and ammunition to the soldiers and nursing the wounded. To reassure himself that the scene in the attic had not been a dream, Hōshimaru searched among them for the women of the night before, but neither the girl to whom he had been especially attracted nor the other four women were to be seen anywhere, though they had always been present before. Only the old woman sat, as usual, in a corner of the room, leaning on her armrest. She deliberately ignored Hōshimaru. He guessed that the five women, busy all night cleaning heads, were resting somewhere during the day. Perhaps even now they were sleeping in the attic. Hōshimaru thought this was probably the case, and he surmised that their absence today meant that they would resume their work tonight.

He waited eagerly for sunset. No doubt the old woman would refuse if he asked her to take him there again, but he no longer needed her to guide him. Indeed, her presence would be a distraction. If he could just slip out the door without her noticing, he would be able to find the way by himself. When he had made up his mind to try, he, too, feigned indifference and avoided her part of the room.

He wondered why he should feel an urgent desire to visit the attic again, and realized that his motive was entirely different from the night before. He was certain, in any case, that his longing was unbefitting the son of a samurai. He tried to tell himself that he was going again to test his courage, but he was vaguely aware that he had another goal in mind. This troubled his conscience, and he suffered from a shame that he could not quite understand.

He was more afraid of awakening the old woman than he was of Aoki Shuzen. Luckily, neither of them noticed as he stole into the corridor, and there were no further complications. He passed through the moonlit garden at the same hour as the night before. Some unseen force drew him in a trance through the door of the storehouse and to the foot of the stairs, but there he stopped and listened for any sounds that might be coming from the upper floor. In fact,

the boy wondered if what he had seen the night before had
not been an illusion: perhaps the old woman had used magic
to make him see something that did not exist. But, as he
stood at the foot of the stairs, water was boiling on the
stove again, and, yes, that unforgettable stench filled the
damp, warm air. Not a sound came from above, but a light
flickered at the top of the stairs. Someone was surely up
there. The night before, he had passed by the kettle of boiling water without knowing its purpose. Now he realized
that it was for washing heads.

The knowledge that everything was real added to his
sense of shame. As he ascended the stairs, he struggled
against something that tried, more powerfully with every
step, to pull him back down. When he reached the top, the
same spectacle as the night before, enacted by the same five
women, unfolded before him. They were not expecting
him tonight, and their surprise showed clearly on their
faces. The three women stopped their work and eyed Hōshimaru suspiciously; but when the oldest of them nodded
politely, the rest, without putting down the heads they
held, followed suit modestly. Doubt had flickered across
their faces for only a moment; they immediately resumed
their silent work. The young noble blushed violently as
the women paid their respects, but he lifted his face haught-
ily and managed to contrive the dignity one expects from
the son of a daimyo. He had not yet learned the art of concealing his embarrassment behind a smile. As the son of a
warlord, he must maintain his dignity at all times—and
especially before women. It must have been an amusing
sight: inwardly abashed, outwardly pompous, the child
stood like a soldier with his shoulders thrown back. To his
relief, the women returned to their work without giving
him a second look. No doubt his coming alone made them
suspicious, but, knowing that it would be impertinent to

reprove him, and that to do so was not their responsibility, they applied themselves diligently to their tasks. Business-like and impassive, they were exactly as they had been the night before. And so was everything else: heads lined up from one end of the room to the other, two lamps burning under the low ceiling, the air smelling of incense and blood. For Hōshimaru, tonight was simply a continuation of last night—the intervening daylight world from which he had escaped seemed like a far-off dream. Only the old woman was missing. Again he was seized by a rapturous intoxication, a violent ecstasy that tore at his heart.

The woman on the right, as before, was using an awl to make a hole in the ear of a "lay-priest head." The girl in the middle, whose duty was to wash the hair, tapped the crown of a head with her comb. She was the girl who had captivated Hōshimaru the previous night. In that province of gory heads, that congregation of death, the girl's youth and freshness must have stood out vividly. Contrasted with the ashen heads, her pink, plump cheeks probably looked all the more alive. Moreover, since the girl's job was to dress the hair, her fingers would have been covered with oil and, against the glossy black hair, no doubt appeared whiter and more voluptuous than they really were. Tonight, too, Hōshimaru saw that mysterious smile playing around her eyes and mouth. When she received a freshly washed head from the woman on the left, she would first cut the cord that bound the topknot; then she would comb the hair carefully, caressingly. Sometimes she would apply a bit of oil, touch up the shaven area with a razor, or, taking an incense burner from the sutra stand at her side, hold the hair over the smoke. Next she would take up a new cord with her right hand, hold one end in her mouth as she gathered the hair together with her left hand, and tie up the topknot again—all exactly as a professional hairdresser might do.

She worked with detachment; but when she scrutinized a finished head, as if she were inspecting the hairstyle, that enigmatic smile would invariably creep across her cheeks.

Probably this smile was simply an expression of the girl's affability. She had formed the habit of smiling pleasantly before others and unconsciously smiled in the same way at a dead person. It would be only natural for her to grow insensitive to the repulsiveness of the heads she worked with, and, as she applied their cosmetics, even to feel affection for them and to respond to them as she would to living persons. But to someone bursting in upon this scene—on one side, the heads, with the agonies of death frozen in their pallid features, and on the other, the young, red lips of the fair girl—her smile, however faint, must have been highly stimulating. Hers was a bewitching beauty, spiced with the bitterness of cruelty. Thus it is not surprising that the twelve-year-old Hōshimaru should have been fascinated by such beauty. Over and above this fascination, however, he experienced an intense emotion beyond the reach of the normal man. According to "Confessions of Dōami," in which the boy's state of mind is described in detail, Hōshimaru envied the head placed before the beautiful girl. He was jealous. But it is important to understand the nature of this jealousy. It is not simply that he envied the head for having the girl dress its hair, shave its pate, or gaze at it with that cruel smile; he wanted to be killed, transformed into a ghastly head with an agonized expression, and manipulated in the girl's hands. Becoming a severed head was a necessary condition. He found no pleasure in imagining himself alive at her side; but if he could become such a head and be set before her in all her charm, how happy he would be!

He was startled and perplexed by the pleasure this strange, illogical fantasy gave him. Until then, he had been the master of his own heart, able to direct its workings as he wished. But in the innermost recesses of his heart was a deep well of a different constitution, beyond the reach of his self-discipline, and the cover of this well had suddenly been lifted. As he placed his hands on the edge and peered into the darkness, he was terrified by the abysmal depth. His feelings were like those of a man who, believing himself to be in robust health, discovers that he has a malignant disease. Hōshimaru did not know where his disease had come from. But he must have sensed, if only vaguely, that there was something morbid in the pleasure that gushed from the secret well in his breast.

Of course he must have realized that he would lose consciousness if he died. His fantasy, therefore—the pleasure he would feel if he were a head placed before the girl—was illogical. It was the fantasy itself that gave him pleasure. He indulged in the fancy that he had become a head without losing consciousness. He tried to imagine that one of the heads brought before the women was his own. When the girl tapped a head with the ridge of her comb, he imagined that he himself was being tapped, and this brought his pleasure to the very summit: his brain grew numb and his body trembled. Among the many different heads, he would concentrate on the ugliest, a head with a sad or pleading expression, or the head of a decrepit old man, and say to himself, "That is me." This gave him far greater pleasure than identifying with the head of a splendid young warrior. In short, he envied the pitiable, repulsive heads more than he did the beautiful ones.

Hōshimaru was an unbending, stouthearted boy. He must have experienced a growing self-hatred as his shameful pleasure became more intense. No doubt he struggled to suppress his excitement. Before long, he summoned all the willpower he possessed and withdrew from the mys-

terious, threatening room that seemed ready to drag him
down into depravity. The long autumn night was still dark
as he hurried back to his room and fell asleep. Hōshimaru's
subsequent anguish is painstakingly related in "Confessions
of Dōami." Three more nights in a row he set out for the
attic. Each time he went, he deluded himself with one excuse or another: it was cowardly to be so frightened; he
was going to test his willpower. But in fact the temptation
of the scene drew him with an almost irresistible force.
During those three days, he was overcome alternately by
self-forgetfulness and remorse. As he descended the stairs
each time, he would repeat to himself his firm resolution:
"I must not come again"; but then, late at night, he would
creep out of bed as if delirious with fever and hurry desperately toward the gate of his secret paradise.

When Hōshimaru arrived at the attic on the third night,
an extraordinary head lay before the girl. It was that of a
young samurai of twenty-one or -two, but, strangely, the
nose was missing. It was an attractive face. The complexion
was wonderfully pale, the freshly shaven places glowed,
and the glossy black hair was as splendid as that which
draped luxuriously over the girl's shoulders and down her
back. No doubt the warrior had been an extremely handsome man. His eyes and mouth were of classic form and
there was a certain delicacy in the firm, well-proportioned,
masculine features. Had there been a fine, straight nose in
the middle, the face would have been the epitome of the
young warrior, just as a master dollmaker might conceive
it. But, for some reason, the nose was missing, as if it had
been sliced off with a sharp blade, bone and all, from the
brow to the upper lip. A pug nose might not have been so
sorely missed; but one would expect to find a sculpturesque
protuberance soaring from the middle of this splendid face.

Instead, that vital feature had been cleanly removed, as if scooped off with a spatula, leaving a flat, crimson wound. As a result the face was uglier and more comical than those of ordinary ugly men. The girl carefully ran her comb through the noseless head's lustrous black hair and retied the topknot; then, as she always did, she gazed at the center of the face, where the nose should have been, and smiled. As usual, the boy was enchanted by her expression, but the surge of emotion he experienced at that moment was far stronger than any he had ever felt before. Juxtaposed with the mutilated head, the girl's face glowed with the pride and joy of the living, the embodiment of flawless beauty. And her smile, precisely because it was so girlish and unaffected, now appeared to be brimming with the most cynical malice, and provided the boy with a wheel on which to spin endless fantasies. He thought he would never tire of gazing at her smiling face. The fantasies it inspired were inexhaustible and, before he was aware of it, had lured his soul away to a land of ambrosial dreams where he himself had become this noseless head and was living with the girl in a world inhabited only by the two of them. This fantasy was very much to his liking. It made him happier than he had ever been before.

His joy turned to rapture; but gradually the smile faded from the girl's cheeks, and for a time the boy stood in a daze, pursuing the traces of his dream. When he saw the girl start to pass the head to the woman on her left, he shattered the deathly silence. "What happened to that one? That head you're holding . . ." Realizing that his voice was quavering, he stopped, then spoke forcefully. "What's going on? That head doesn't have a nose."

"No, sir." Placing her hands, glossy with oil, on the headboard in front of her, she assumed the respectful posture customary when addressing a noble. In doing so she glanced up at the boy's face for a moment, but immediately lowered her head and made a graceful, deferential bow.

"He must have been a fool to get his nose cut off," said the boy. A husky laugh, more like an old man's cough than the laugh of a child, welled up from his throat and echoed strangely through the attic.

"Why was he cut there?"

"But, sir, this is a woman-head."

"A woman's head?"

"No, sir." Perhaps at her age she was uncomfortable speaking to men; perhaps she had sensed from the boy's demeanor, or from the way he had blurted out his questions, that there was something abnormal about him. In any case, she kept her eyes lowered as she explained, timidly and reluctantly. "A woman-head is not a woman's head. I do not know much about it, but I am told that a warrior in battle is not always able to take the head of an enemy he has killed and carry it around with him. In such cases, he takes only the nose so that he can go back later to find the head itself."

As Hōshimaru pressed his questions, the girl bowed her head lower and lower and replied in the fewest words possible. He wanted to know, for example, why it was called a "woman-head." This was because if only a nose was brought back, no one could tell whether it came from a man or a woman. Generally, noseless heads were not desirable. But on the battlefield, a warrior who had taken three or four heads could not possibly carry them all around with him. Instead, he took the noses and used them to find the heads after the battle. Nose cutting was permitted only when absolutely necessary, she said, and so, as a rule, very few woman-heads came in. This was the first one she had handled in the current siege. Hōshimaru was able to coax this much information from her, and no more.

To quote from "Confessions of Dōami":

My master told me, "Nothing is so strange as the heart of man. If I had not met that girl and had never seen a woman-head, I should never have given myself over to such shameful activities. My disgrace arose from the memory of that girl's face, so deeply imbedded in my heart that I could not forget it morning or night. I wanted to bring in another woman-head and see her smiling face again. Having resolved on this, I was overcome with impatience, and one night I stole out of the castle to the enemy camp."

In Which Hōshimaru Takes a Nose at the Enemy Camp and Proves His Courage

Several obstacles stood between Hōshimaru and the realization of his desire to see another noseless head placed before the girl in the attic. First of all, he could not depend on someone else to bring in a woman-head; he would have to get one himself. Yet he was forbidden to go to the battlefield. Even if he were able to slip out of the castle, there would be another hurdle: he would have to locate a prominent enemy warrior, wrestle him to the ground, and cut off his head and nose. He would have to conceal the fact that he had taken the head himself and send it to the girl under someone else's name. To earn distinction on the battlefield, it was necessary to have a witness, but Hōshimaru's objective was not to distinguish himself. It was simply to see the girl smiling again at a noseless head. The easiest solution would be to hunt out a suitable corpse among those scattered on the battlefield, cut off its head, and either invent a witness or bribe some foot soldiers; but this his warrior's conscience would not allow. The son of a samurai house could not countenance such a cowardly plan. He must kill an enemy warrior by himself, cut off the head, and remove the nose. Hōshimaru wrestled with his problem in secret. He had to come up with a plan quickly, for the women in the attic might be replaced.

As Hōshimaru nurtured his strange hopes and plans, the two armies continued their desperate battle at the critical boundary of the keep and the second citadel. Flushed with the prospect of impending victory, the Yakushiji troops surged over the stone walls, battered down the gates, and rushed in a black knot into the keep, only to be stopped by the frantic defenders, pushed back to the second citadel, and thrown into confusion. Angry shouts, gunfire, screams, and the dull roar of armies rushing now this way, now that; all day the din of slaughter and destruction echoed like thunder in Hōshimaru's ears. There was little hope that the redoubtable Ojika Castle could hold out much longer. Aoki Shuzen now wore a bandage on his thigh where a spear had caught him; he had been wounded twice in the arm, but he bore up under his injuries and went on fighting. He looked in on Hōshimaru only rarely, and each time, as he withdrew to return to battle, he would say with a tragic look, "Are you ready, Master? When the time comes, do not forget what I have always told you." He seemed to mean that Hōshimaru should be prepared to die bravely at any moment by cutting himself open. Meanwhile, the women, even the old one who had been his guide, were busy nursing the wounded and carrying the dead. Sometimes they worked all night.

But if the fate of the castle and his own life hung by a thread, Hōshimaru hardly gave it a thought. What mattered to him now was that he could do as he pleased, thanks to the pandemonium within the castle. It would not be difficult to slip out unobserved. The only problem was how to infiltrate the enemy camp. The second night after his strange experience in the attic, Hōshimaru quietly descended the hill behind the keep and took a secret path that led him outside the castle walls. He reasoned that because most of the enemy were concentrated inside the second and third citadels, the guard would be relaxed at the main camp beyond the outer moat. With few warriors about, he would be certain to find his chance if he followed the path and emerged directly behind the enemy headquarters. His heart pounded and he trembled with anticipation, like a warrior going into battle for the first time. The girl's lovely smile and a multitude of noseless heads danced before his eyes.

It was about two o'clock in the morning when the boy started down the path. The moon that had cast its pale glow on his nightly visits to the attic rested now on the ridge of Mount Ojika and inscribed his shadow sharply on the ground. He held a thin veil over his head so that he would look like a woman fleeing the castle; as he walked he saw its tremulous shadow float across the ground like a jellyfish.

Having sustained the siege for two months and quartered more than twenty thousand men, the enemy camp must have been well equipped. The castle on Mount Ojika stood at the edge of a mountainous area, on a promontory that thrust like a peninsula into the plain; the enemy had formed their camp in the shape of a horseshoe around the skirt of this peninsula. They had erected a bamboo fence around the camp, lit watch fires every ten or twenty yards, and built lookout towers here and there just inside the fence. Finally, they had set up a number of temporary board shelters that served as barracks, in which the army, from the general on down, slept. Hōshimaru followed his path through the open top of the horseshoe and skirted the back of the enemy camp until he reached the bottom of the horseshoe. He was now behind the camp headquarters, which faced the front gate of the castle. Breaking through the bamboo fence, he stole undetected into the enclosure. Of course, under normal conditions it would not have been so easy to infiltrate the enemy camp; but, as he had expected, most of the enemy soldiers were at their posts inside the third and second citadels, leaving the camp shorthanded and the lookouts off their guard.

The boy was familiar with life in a castle, but tonight he was seeing the arrangement of a field camp for the first time and went far toward satisfying his curiosity just by slipping inside the fence. Realizing that his disguise would only invite suspicion inside the camp, he folded the veil he had been wearing and put it in the breast of his kimono. Then, as quickly and lightly as a bird in flight, he darted from building to building, hiding in the dark shadows carved out by the brilliant moon. He paused under the eaves of each building and peered inside. Fortunately for the boy, the light of the watch fires was offset by the moonlight and looked like pale white smoke. The indiscriminate radiance of the moon cast a gold reflection on the earth and imparted a blinding phosphorescence to every object, however small, in the pellucid night air of autumn. This extraordinary brilliance obscured the lookouts' view. The boy crept past a group of crouching guards as they huddled around their fire, and went directly under a lookout tower, clinging to the shadow that the tower threw like a sash on the ground; but no one challenged him. As the castle defenders had been driven into the keep, the lookouts had no doubt relaxed their vigilance and gone to sleep. Even if someone had seen him they probably would have mistaken him for a page boy enchanted by the moon.

Each barrack was enclosed by a camp curtain bearing

the crest of the occupant. A signboard stood at each entrance, and flags, banners, spears, and the like were deposited inside the curtains. As Hōshimaru examined these quarters one by one, he chanced upon an especially handsome curtain bearing a distinctive crest. He stopped in his tracks: it was the crest of Yakushiji Danjō Masataka, and the curtain, he knew, must enclose the headquarters of the enemy general. Lifting the curtain and drawing himself up against the plank wall of the barrack, he listened intently for a moment, but heard nothing. Then, circling behind the building, he found a stable with five or six tethered horses, apparently belonging to the general. Even they were sleeping peacefully. Hōshimaru sensed that he had been presented with an opportunity to perform unimagined deeds of glory. His objective had been to take a woman-head, not the head of the general. But, if he let this providential moment pass, he would be unworthy of his samurai heritage. Because the general's standard and banners were stowed here, it was just possible that Masataka had not joined the besieging forces, but was asleep in an inner room of this barrack. If all went well and the boy took the commander in chief's head, he would accomplish a feat of unparalleled distinction. The thought was a spur to his adventurous scheme. With the composure and courage of a grown man, he quietly slid open the back door. In an instant, he was feeling his way along the wooden floor of the corridor toward, he guessed, the inner chambers. The surroundings were pitch-dark, but with the help of the moonlight that stole through knotholes and between the planks in the wall, he found his way to the end of the corridor and finally to a door. Through a narrow opening, the light of a flame seeped from the room beyond. The boy slid the door open about a foot. The interior was partitioned into two areas. That which Hōshimaru could see appeared to be an antechamber, with two sleeping pages of about his own age. A screen separated the antechamber from the inner space beyond; a lamp was burning behind the screen. Taking care not to disturb the sleeping pages, Hōshimaru tiptoed through the antechamber, crouched in the shadow of the screen, and fixed his gaze on the face of the warrior who slept within. Though the barrack was of rough plank construction, the room was large, and near the pillow was a makeshift alcove in which hung a scroll depicting Hachiman, the god of war. An image of the ferocious Fudō Myōō, god of fire, had been installed in a portable shrine beside the bed. The accessories, the long sword, the armor, the sword rack, and the lavish furnishings of gold and silver lacquer, left no doubt: these were not the quarters of an ordinary samurai. The man's hair, moreover, was bound in the style reserved for generals; his head rested on a lustrous, black-lacquer pillow, and he wore a damask silk nightgown. Hōshimaru had no prior knowledge of Masataka's age or appearance. This man seemed to be about fifty years old. He had a broad forehead and a refined, oval face with smooth skin and elegant features, and in repose looked more like a courtier than a samurai. Most warriors of his years would have had firm, sunburned skin and borne some traces of the battlefield; but the complexion of this sleeping face, though rather dark, resembled the surface of brightly polished wood and had the delicate texture of the finest paper vellum. This was not the skin of a warrior who spent his days on horseback buffeted by rain and wind, but rather that of an aristocrat who had been sheltered as a child and knew nothing but the courtly pleasures of poetry and music.

Indeed, Yakushiji Danjō Masataka was a powerful man, though technically only a vassal of the Hatakeyama clan. Since his father's time, the influence of his family had surpassed that of the Hatakeyama and occasionally, even as an undervassal, he had been able to direct the will of the Muromachi shogunate. Largely due to his father's abilities, he had risen to this special status. His own military achievements had not been particularly glorious. Rather, he had used the favorable position achieved by his father as a springboard and, with his own eloquence, wit, and shrewdness, had ingratiated himself with his superiors and profited by an age in which subordinates often dominated their masters. Thus, though a daimyo in name, he was simply an epigone of the gentility who had assumed the airs of a court adherent. In those days, many of the Kyoto samurai, from members of the shogunate on down, gradually came under the influence of the court and began to affect the ways of nerveless aristocrats, and so it is not surprising that Masataka was more accomplished in poetry than in warfare. He had come to this siege in person as commander in chief but, trusting in the advantage his forces had won, slept comfortably now in his barrack. Such was the man upon whose sleeping face Hōshimaru gazed.

The boy sensed that something was lacking in this man who, he concluded, must be Masataka himself. True, the man had the dignity and gravity befitting a prominent daimyo, but he seemed a bit too mild. He lacked the majesty one would expect in the chief of a military clan and commander of an army of twenty thousand. The boy had imagined a general with the same qualities that he had seen in his father Terukuni, Lord of Musashi, and in Ikkansai of Mount Ojika, a body like tempered steel and a bold face burning with the desire for conquest. This delicate figure could be dispatched too easily—not much of a challenge, the boy thought. But this was no cause for dismay or disappointment to Hōshimaru. He might have felt something of the sort had he been out to demonstrate his courage or to perform great feats; but he was looking at the sleeping face from a different point of view. In the center of the face was a shapely, slender, delicate, and aristocratic nose. From where he stood, Hōshimaru could peer directly into the nostrils of the slightly upturned nose and judge, from the long, lean strip separating the nostrils, that the flesh was thin. As is characteristic of aristocratic noses, the bridge arched slightly and the contour of the bone was faintly evident under the skin. If he were to slice this nose from this face, the thrill excited by the destruction would be scarcely less than that inspired by the woman-head in the attic. There it had been the head of a handsome young warrior. But this head was attached to the torso of the enemy commander, inadequate as he may have been, and was elegant, delicate, and refined, more than compensating for the defect of being middle-aged. No, surely this nose was even more seductive than the other, enough to fill the boy, who had derived such pleasure from the scene in the attic, with longing.

As he gazed, the light from the small oil lamp swayed and trembled in the draft. With each flicker, the shadow that the nose threw across the sleeping face swayed, too. Sometimes, depending on the movement of the flame, the entire nose would be swallowed in darkness. Suddenly the nose would reappear, then disappear. It was as if the capricious light were trying to incite the boy. The nose itself urged him on by looking as if it had already been sliced off. It seemed anxious to be severed as quickly as possible. Once again Hōshimaru visualized the girl's enigmatic smile. He would turn this face into a noseless head, place it before her knees, expose it to her gaze—there could be no greater pleasure.

Hōshimaru was heavy and strong for his age, and confident of his ability with a sword. Abruptly he kicked the

sleeping man's pillow and, before his adversary could reach
for a sword, jumped on his chest as he tried to sit up, strad-
dled him, and pierced his throat with a single thrust. The
short sword, a gift from his father Terukuni, had been
made by the famous Kanemitsu, but the boy's skill was
even more impressive than the weapon. Having struck
home with one thrust, he extracted the sword and rose so
quickly that he was scarcely touched by the spurting blood.
He was surprised by his own skill and dexterity. The man
had not even had time to cry out. Hōshimaru had seen the
panic-filled eyes and the mouth, open and ready to speak and
then, an instant later, the face of death, frozen, the features
twisted in agony. At that moment Hōshimaru glimpsed
the flash of a blade close behind him. The two boys who
had been sleeping in the antechamber had drawn their
swords simultaneously and rushed him; but, his confidence
bolstered by the feat he had just performed, Hōshimaru
dodged to one side and bounded up into the alcove. There
he stood ready, with the scroll of Hachiman behind him.
This position put him at an advantage, as half the space in
front of the alcove was taken up by the corpse, the portable
shrine, and the bedside furnishings, so that the approaching enemies were forced to one side. The pages were clearly
disconcerted by the sight of their dead master and by the
realization that the killer was a stripling of about their own
age. As he leaped into the alcove and waited for his pursuers
with all the poise of a veteran, Hōshimaru must have looked
to them like a demon that had sprung from the earth. In
spite of their initial vigor, the pages cautiously circled their
master's body, taking care not to step on it, and inched toward the alcove.

Their sword tips aligned, the two boys advanced together to the edge of the alcove, but, as they were about
to enter, the more timid one fell back. Hōshimaru watched

the movements of the one in front. The moment the page
set his foot on the sill of the dais, Hōshimaru dashed forward and struck a blow with his sword. The page stepped
back, startled by this savage attack from a boy who had
been standing transfixed in a corner six feet away. The
dais, low as it was, gave Hōshimaru the advantage. Seeing
that his first blow had cut deeply into the page's shoulder,
Hōshimaru embraced him tightly and stabbed him again in
the side. With blood pouring from his wounds, the boy
crumpled slowly, like a sinking ship. Even before the first
page hit the floor, Hōshimaru attacked the second. Overawed, this wretched boy had no will to fight, but stood
his ground out of determination to follow his master in
death. Averting his eyes from the flash of Hōshimaru's
sword, he parried two or three times; but it was a resigned,
apologetic, tearful sort of resistance. Hōshimaru struck the
sword from his hand, kicked him down, and stabbed him
in the chest.

With the two pages disposed of, he knelt beside the general's corpse and, grasping the topknot in his left hand,
began to cut off the head with his right. Just then he heard
the footsteps of several men running toward him down the
corridor. Quick as he had been, the boy must have consumed fifteen or twenty minutes to accomplish so much.
Apparently no one had been in attendance near the inner
chamber, and only now had warriors in a room some distance away been startled by the noise and come running.
Hōshimaru had no time to lose. But it proved more difficult
to cut the head neatly from the body than it had been to
stab a living man, and he panicked when he heard voices
approaching from behind. His blade was stuck in the neck
bone when someone burst into the antechamber. If he were
to escape, he must go now. So far, his plan had succeeded
miraculously, but in the end he would have to abandon his

objective or be cut to pieces. Gnashing his teeth in frustration, he pulled out the sword. But then, for whatever reason, he sliced off the corpse's nose. The lump of flesh tumbled to the floor. Snatching it up in a reflex, he pushed open a sliding door and fled.

It often seems, when one reads the life of a great hero, that heaven has bestowed some special protection on his fate, enabling him to venture into situations far beyond the experience of ordinary men and to escape untouched. Hōshimaru's exploit is such an example. Perhaps he cut off the nose to vent his frustration; or perhaps he wanted to accomplish at least part of his objective; or again, perhaps the audacious boy acted in the end out of panic. There is no way of knowing. But whatever the case may be, if he had not taken the nose with him when he fled, he probably would have been caught. This is no more than conjecture; but when the warriors reached the bedchamber and discovered that something important was missing from their master's face, a few of them surely went after the culprit, but the rest, jumping to the conclusion that the nose had been chopped off accidentally (for they would never have guessed that the assailant took it with him), probably poked about the room in search of a piece of their master's face. At first only two or three men chased Hōshimaru, and apparently they mistook the boy running in front of them for one of their own pages who had awakened and come with them. Hōshimaru just got away from the room by a hair, and before he could cross the outer fence he heard trumpet shells and drums being sounded in watchtowers on every side. Jolted from their dreams, men poured out of the barracks. The camp was in an uproar, but the confusion was to Hōshimaru's advantage. Weaving a path among the steadily multiplying torches, he finally pulled a burning brand from a watch fire and waved it about. The boy was clever enough to realize that his figure would be obscured if he held a flame in his own hand. Reaching the outside of the compound safely, he discarded the torch and, after running six or seven hundred yards, put on his veil and dissolved into the boundless light of the moon.

In Which Both Sides Are Perplexed, and the Yakushiji Forces Raise the Siege

According to the history books, Yakushiji Danjō Masataka fell ill during the assault on Ojika Castle in the Tenth Month of 1549, raised the siege and withdrew to Kyoto, where he died ten days later at his mansion on Aburakōji. It is clear from "Confessions of Dōami" and "The Dream of a Night" that this account is untrue, but at the time only a few members of the attacking force—and, in the castle, only Hōshimaru himself—knew the real story.

It would seem that within moments of Hōshimaru's escape a fire, visible from the castle, broke out in the camp. Only one barrack burned, and the fire was quickly brought under control. It seems likely that someone in the camp was prudent enough to set a fire deliberately to provide a plausible explanation for the commotion. When all is said and done, the murder of the commander in chief was a consequence of dereliction; and, to make matters worse, the assassin had been allowed to escape. The embarrassment of the high command must have been extreme. But first and foremost, a frantic search for the nose was conducted. A missing nose was far more difficult to deal with than a missing head. Imagawa Yoshimoto underestimated his enemy and lost his life at the battle of Okehazama, but in time his head was returned, with the nose, of course, firmly in place. It was a double humiliation, however, for

Masataka's head to have been left behind and the nose taken, and the news could hardly be announced to the camp. And so it seems that, as an expedient, the leaders imposed silence on those who had viewed the death scene and ascribed the drums and trumpets to the fire.

But even if the troops were taken in by this strategy, the truth might come from the enemy. An envoy would arrive with the nose on a platter and say, "Something precious belonging to Lord Masataka has unexpectedly fallen into our hands. No doubt you have need of it, and so we respectfully return it herewith." The senior retainers in the Yakushiji camp were terrified that something of the sort might occur. When dawn broke they relaxed the assault and watched to see what the castle would do, but no message came. As the attack subsided, the besieged castle, too, was oddly silent, which made the senior retainers all the more anxious. They began to suspect a plot. Some suggested that whoever had penetrated the general's bedroom was not an agent of the castle, but a thief, or perhaps someone with a personal grudge against the lord. If the attacker had been a samurai, he would not have perpetrated that senseless prank of cutting off the nose. This argument made sense, but others believed that a samurai from the castle had indeed taken the nose, not having had time to cut off the head, and that the enemy intended to use it to humiliate them.

Even as the Yakushiji leaders were trying to fathom the castle's intentions, the castle forces, too, felt uneasy, not knowing why the triumphant besiegers had suddenly eased their attack. The defenders had believed, as they fought, that they could only be saved by a political change in Kyoto, but there had been no reports of anything of the sort. The besiegers had pressed their attack until the fall of the castle was imminent, and there was no reason for them to pull back now; but they had been strangely cautious since morning. They no longer sounded the attack drums or even returned the castle's gunfire, but instead firmed up their defenses and remained silent, all for no apparent reason. There had been a fire in the enemy camp the night before. Maybe something was seriously wrong. Spies were sent out but learned nothing of significance. Something was surely amiss, and so Ikkansai met with his senior officers to try to puzzle it out, but no one could offer more than random guesses; each had his own theory, and no headway was made. Someone argued that the castle should launch a desperate attack; but that would be dangerous, others responded, because there was no telling what secret designs the enemy might have. In time they would see how things stood, and the castle forces would sit still until the enemy made a move. At length the day drew to a close.

While the armies on both sides were falling prey to demons of their own creation, Hōshimaru was in anguish over his failure of the night before. Though at the time he had not been certain that the man he killed was the enemy commander in chief, he was finally convinced when morning came and the attack suddenly blunted. But he was not about to go gleefully telling others of his deed. Children often throw grown-ups into an uproar with some innocent, impulsive prank that leads to undreamed-of complications. In such cases, everyone would be spared a great deal of trouble if the child would only explain that he himself had sparked the affair; but, afraid of a scolding, or reluctant to speak up once things have come to such a pass, they feign ignorance and hope that no one will be the wiser. Hōshimaru's feelings were something akin to this. If he had come forward and acknowledged that he had caused the change in the enemy's attitude by his exploit of the night before, the defenders would instantly have regained their spirits and been spared needless anxiety. Hōshimaru itched to speak up when he considered how brilliantly he had conducted himself and how his father and Ikkansai would praise him if they knew what he had accomplished at such a tender age; but he was terrified by the thought that his feat had been incidental, and that the shameful motivation underlying it would be exposed. Anyway, who would believe him if he tried to take credit without evidence or witnesses? Had he presented himself the moment he returned to the keep, he might have been believed; but in fact, before burrowing under his covers, he had been careful to destroy the evidence by hurling his bloodstained clothes into the great watchfire. Now the only proof he had was the nose itself, wrapped in paper and hidden in his breast; but if he presented it, he would give away his vital secret.

What preoccupied Hōshimaru most was an intense regret that his plan of the night before had miscarried at the critical moment. No doubt the enemy had learned their lesson and would be more vigilant, making it impossible for him to steal into the camp again so easily. Now and then, after making sure that he was alone, he would take the nose from his breast and fall into a reverie. The corpse's face at the moment he cut off the nose was deeply etched in his imagination, and the image grew more vivid each time he took out the little lump of flesh. But if he only had the head itself! He longed to go after it. The body of the commander in chief would, no doubt, be lying in state even now in that inner chamber. Hōshimaru pictured the room, then the stately corpse's elegant, sleek face, and finally the cavity in the center of the face. Like a rare object of great value, the image excited his desire to possess. But now that the fighting was over, the women in the attic had ceased their work. Even if he could steal the head and bring it to the castle, he had forever lost all hope of placing it before the girl. He could, however, steal glances at her as she sat among the women who, with nothing to occupy them any longer, gathered in his room again to form a circle around the old woman and chat from morning to night.

But there is nothing so hopeless and vulnerable as a boy's secret, unrequited love for an older woman. Without realizing it, the girl had ignited the flame of passion in Hōshimaru's breast and inaugurated his outrageous sexual life. Yet Hōshimaru felt only a distant, dreamlike adoration and had virtually no direct contact with her. As he mingled with the gossipers, he took comfort in being able to listen to her voice and to gaze furtively at the smile that crept across her cheeks. But the smile inspired secret fantasies of the attic scene and, though it was no more than the friendly smile of a good-natured girl, Hōshimaru saw cruelty in it and was enraptured. He was saddened to hear the women say, "The siege seems to be over," or, "Apparently the castle will be spared." Each day the siege continued was another day he could be near the girl, and he did not want it to end.

The two armies faced each other in trepidation for four days, but on the fifth the attackers finally raised the siege, folded their camp, and withdrew. To the last, the senior Yakushiji retainers were unable to find their master's nose and had no idea who the assailant was. Perhaps they lost their nerve. Announcing "Lord Masataka's sudden illness," they carried the corpse away in a palanquin. By that time, word had spread through both armies that something was wrong with the commander in chief. Many guessed that he was already dead, though no one doubted the rumors that ascribed the cause to illness. But if the soldiers bearing the palanquin had taken one look at the face of the "patient," they would have been startled. The bacterium of the disease that causes one's nose to fall off had been introduced to Japan at about this time, along with tobacco, but surely had not spread very far yet.

This concludes the anecdotes from the Lord of Musashi's childhood, the period when he was called Hōshimaru. "Confessions of Dōami" adds a final note:

My master said, "Kawagoe Jimbei covered the enemy's retreat from the second and third citadels. Our side sallied from the keep at once to harass them as they withdrew, but Ikkansai restrained his men, saying that a samurai does not profit from another's misfortune. If Masataka were ill, we must let him go. Everyone in the castle had been resigned to certain death. Now they rejoiced. Banquets were spread in the turrets; everyone was drunk on celebratory sake. I do not know where the women hostages went. Perhaps, since the siege was over, they bid farewell and returned to their native places. I wanted to see the girl once more but, though I searched everywhere, I never found her. I learned that she was called Teru, daughter of Lord Ida of Suruga. If only there were another siege, I thought, I could meet her again. I hoped that someday the enemy would renew their attack."

"If only there were another siege I could meet her again." The boy sounds like Oshichi, the greengrocer's daughter, who set fire to her house so that she could rejoin her lover at the neighborhood temple. What a ludicrous thought.

Book III

❀❀❀❀❀

In Which Hōshimaru Comes of Age,
and Concerning Lady Kikyō

Hōshimaru came of age on the eleventh day of the First
Month, in the spring of 1552, when he was fifteen years
old. He was still in the castle on Mount Ojika, serving as
Ikkansai's page. The coming-of-age ceremony is described
in "The Dream of a Night" with that scrupulous attention
characteristic of women writers; but it is a verbose account,
and there is no need to go into such detail here. The ceremony was held in a room at Ikkansai's mansion, the nun
Myōkaku writes, and Hōshimaru's father, Terukuni, Lord
of Musashi, came from his domain to place the symbolic
cap on his son's head. Hōshimaru was five feet, two inches
tall at the time; when he donned the long-corded cap and
walked behind his father, it was apparent that father and
son were the same height.

The reader should take note that Hōshimaru was five
feet, two inches tall at the age of fifteen. It is not clear what
the average height for men was during the Period of Civil
Wars, but probably a height of five-two was not remarkable for a lad of his age. Myōkaku, author of "The Dream
of a Night," often comments on his appearance as an adult.
For example, "My lord's face was the color of iron, and his
physique surpassed that of any other man; though he was
not tall, he was thickset"; and elsewhere, "The light in his
eyes was sharp, his cheekbones were high and his lips thick,
and his face was large for a man of his height." From this

we can surmise that he did not grow much taller after coming of age. Perhaps he inherited his short stature from Terukuni, who was no taller than his young son. But it is not difficult to imagine the awe inspired by that tremendous face, so large in proportion to his height.

And so Hōshimaru assumed the name Terukatsu, taking one character from his father's sobriquet, and the honorary title "Vice-Governor of Kawachi"; and as early as the summer of that year, during Ikkansai's siege of Mizukuri Castle, he made a splendid debut on the battlefield. Not only did he take the head of the enemy general Hotta Mizaemon, he was the first to scale the wall and leap into the castle. Urging his soldiers on with shouts of "Don't let Terukatsu be killed," Ikkansai finally took the castle. It is said that Terukuni, in residence at Mount Tamon, wept with joy when he heard of his son's prowess from Aoki Shuzen. Ikkansai, too, had warm praise for Terukatsu's bravery that day; but it seems that privately he voiced his anxiety to an attendant: "He will be a man to fear. What will become of the House of Tsukuma after I am gone?" And so he must already have been on his guard, recognizing that Terukatsu was not only skilled in battle but exceptionally clever and bold as well. According to Terukatsu himself (as recorded in "Confessions of Dōami"), Ikkansai's eldest son, Oribenoshō Norishige, also took part in this siege. Norishige was two years older than Terukatsu, but greatly inferior in looks, physique, and ability. This could hardly have gone unnoticed by his father Ikkansai, whose inner distress was obvious, and Terukatsu resolved not to incur the distrust of either father or son.

But it is not the object of this tale to give an account of Terukatsu the battlefield hero. The details given above are recorded in the *Tsukuma War Chronicles* chapter entitled "Concerning the Fall of Mizukuri Castle," and in various other chronicles. The question that remains is: what had become of Terukatsu's mysterious pleasure, the monstrous fantasies, the desire to pursue a "secret paradise," that the woman-head had inspired in him as a boy? One would think, on the basis of his spectacular debut in battle, that the sordid memory had disappeared without a trace from the heart of the young warrior and been replaced by a fiercely burning ambition. In fact, all boys probably experience once or twice something akin to the mysterious secret pleasure he tasted as a boy. But occasionally, when a boy is placed in conducive surroundings and relives those feelings again and again, the secret pleasure will eat its way into his heart and take root as a morbid perversion that governs his entire sexual life. Accordingly, Terukatsu might never have discovered the existence of that "secret paradise" had he not seen a woman-head as a boy. Or even had he discovered it just once, his sexual appetites would surely not have been so warped if the childhood wound had never again been prodded. After all, the son of a daimyo in the Period of Civil Wars did not lead the tranquil life of aristocratic young men today, and he would hardly have had time to nurture such wild, depraved fantasies. It would be safe to say, then, that the young Terukatsu had no choice but to abstain from his shameful pleasure for a time and devote himself single-mindedly to winning a reputation on the battlefield. To his misfortune, the woman who was to reignite his unsavory proclivities entered the stage at this point.

Lady Kikyō, the wife of Tsukuma Oribenoshō Norishige, was the daughter of the same Yakushiji Danjō Masataka who "succumbed to illness" after the siege of Ojika Castle. She went as Norishige's bride in 1551, two years after the siege, at the age of fifteen; she was thus one year younger than Norishige and a year older than Terukatsu. She is described in "The Dream of a Night":

> Being a wellborn lady from the capital, she knew the ways of poetry and music; nor even Yang Kuei-fei of far Cathay or Princess Sotoori of our own land could have matched the pearly beauty of her petal eyebrows and rosy lips. . . .

This string of clichés does not make clear how beautiful she may actually have been. That she was exceptionally attractive is probably true, for it was said that she was in no way inferior to her mother, daughter of the Middle Counselor of the Chrysanthemum Pavilion, who was rumored to be a great beauty; and for this reason Norishige, a born amorist, had long been hoping for a match.

It was the advocacy of the shogunate that brought the marriage negotiations to a successful conclusion. When in 1549 Yakushiji Danjō Masataka had surrounded the castle on Mount Ojika with a huge army and nearly forced Ikkansai to commit ritual suicide, it had been the culmination of many years of incessant warfare between the Yakushiji and Tsukuma clans. There could be no peace in the land as long as these two houses of roughly equal strength continued their fighting, and the feud might well lead to widespread disorder. Accordingly, the Muromachi shogunate seized the opportunity presented by Masataka's death to intervene; the two sides put their long years of enmity behind them and the marriage was arranged to mark their reconciliation. On the Yakushiji side, Lady Kikyō's brother Masahide had succeeded as head of the family. He knew that his father Masataka had not died from illness but had been cut down in his barracks by an interloper, and that his corpse had suffered an intolerable humiliation. As a consequence, Masahide's hatred and distrust of the Tsukuma clan were unabated, but he put on a good face for the occasion and accepted the shogunate's proposal with a show of gratitude. On the Tsukuma side, no one but Terukatsu knew the true circumstances of Masataka's death, and so we may be sure that the entire clan, having no reason to doubt Masahide's intentions, rejoiced over the reconciliation and marriage. And the bridegroom, Norishige, rejoiced most of all.

In the Third Month of 1553—something more than a year after the wedding—Ikkansai died in his sickbed, according to the *Tsukuma War Chronicles* and other records. In retrospect, this death too looks suspicious, though neither "Confessions of Dōami" or "The Dream of a Night" suggests that there was any mystery about it. He died of dysentery at the age of fifty-three, they say, and this is plausible enough; yet in the *Tsukuma War Chronicles*, the account of the cause and progress of the disease is more detailed than usual, and somehow does not ring true. But rather than probe any deeper into the circumstances of Ikkansai's death, let us proceed to the next incident.

In the fall of 1554, Tsukuma Oribenoshō Norishige, having received reports of an insurrection by his vassal Yokowa Buzen, master of Tsukigata Castle, led a cavalry of seven thousand to retake the fortress. Terukatsu accompanied Norishige as his attendant. On the tenth day of the Eighth Month, in the midst of battle, Norishige drew up his horse in a shady grove about a mile from the front gate of the castle. He was directing his troops from this vantage point, when suddenly a bullet flew past the bridge of his nose, missing it by a hair. With a gasp, Norishige instinctively clapped his hands to his nose. Instantly there was a second bullet, which this time very nearly swept the nose from his face. A blister formed on the ridge of his nose, as if it had been burned by a sparkler, and a trace of blood seeped through the broken skin. Terukatsu, who had been standing in front of the horse, quickly shielded his commander and, his eyes darting about the battlefield, led him toward cover in the grove. Norishige, being the sniper's target, was naturally alarmed; but anxiety seized Terukatsu as well. Norishige was alarmed because he believed that an attempt had been made on his life, but Terukatsu suspected that such was not the case. The sniper had obviously been aiming for the general's nose. Since both shots had been fired from the same direction, and the second had come closer to the mark than the first, they could not have been stray bullets. The trajectory had been parallel to Norishige's face as he sat on his horse—in other words, at a right angle to the bulge of his nose, surely not the angle an assassin would choose. But these were not the only grounds for Terukatsu's suspicions. He had been a witness once before, when a similar incident had befallen Ikkansai. It had occurred about two months before the onset of Ikkansai's fatal illness, during the battle of Chigusagawa, in the Twelfth Month of 1552. On that occasion, too, the bullet had traced a horizontal line in front of Ikkansai's face, but as there had been only a single shot, only Terukatsu had given it much notice. Confronted now with an almost identical situation, Terukatsu grew more and more anxious. Someone had wanted Ikkansai's nose and now was after the nose of his son and heir, Norishige. In the midst of the shouts and dust of the furious battle, Terukatsu suddenly recalled the long-forgotten mischief of his childhood. Masataka's noseless death face, the woman-head, the beautiful girl's enigmatic smile as she gazed at the head—no doubt these phantoms flitted before his eyes like flashes of lightning. Simultaneously he remembered his duty. The phantoms threatened to lure his soul into transports of ecstasy, but he dispelled them with a wave of his hand and tried to determine who had fired the shots. The warriors in Tsukigata Castle, resigned to certain death, had come slashing forth and had set upon the besieging army in a frantic last attempt to crush them. The field was transformed into the scene of a brutal melee as battle lines crisscrossed and hand-to-hand fighting spread nearly to the threshold of Norishige's headquarters; but Terukatsu at once turned his gaze in the direction from which the bullets had been fired and picked out the figure of a samurai standing about two hundred yards away and peering toward him. He wore a fine, black-lacquer breastplate decorated in gold. Terukatsu knew intuitively that he was the sniper. The man had been poised to fire a third shot, but instead he flung the musket away and ran.

As the distance between them was too great for Terukatsu to overtake the man, he stayed out of sight and tailed him. Terukatsu drew within six feet when the samurai reached the edge of the moat at the front gate of the castle.

"Stop." He hurled the word abruptly from behind.

"Yes?" The man slowly turned around and took a step back. Seen at close range, he was a fine-looking samurai. He wore a richly decorated helmet, and the glittering design on his breastplate was the character for "dragon" written large in gold lacquer.

"Identify yourself. I am Terukatsu, Vice-Governor of Kawachi, eldest son of Kiryū Terukuni, Lord of Musashi."

"There is no point in giving my name."

"Coward, why did you use a musket?"

"I did not."

"Shut up! I saw you drop it and run."

"You've mistaken me for someone else."

"All right! Deny it if you like."

Even before Terukatsu spoke, the point of his spear was

flashing at the "dragon." His objective was to immobilize the mysterious samurai with a deep wound and take him alive. At first, the man regarded Terukatsu as a mere child, but then the spearhead was upon him like a swarm of locusts, and after just three or four parries he had been overpowered and stabbed in the leg through the braided cord on the skirt of his armor. Terukatsu then stabbed him in the upper right arm and fell astride him. He heard a gasp of despair and frustration from below.

"Your name!"

"No. Cut off my head."

"I'm going to take you alive."

When the warrior heard the words "take you alive," he began to writhe and thrash violently, in spite of his wounds. Terukatsu looked around for someone to help him, but all he could see was a vast cloud of dust, and beyond it, shadowy masses forming, then breaking, like waves on a boiling sea. In the interval, the pinned warrior clutched Terukatsu's sash with his right hand, drew his short sword with his left and began thrusting indiscriminately. Without help, Terukatsu could no longer hope to take him prisoner. Reluctantly, he pressed the point of his blade to the man's throat.

"I'll give you your wish. Tell me your name," Terukatsu demanded one last time. But the man snapped, "Be done with it!"

Saying no more, he pressed his lips tightly and shut his eyes. I would have asked who sent him after Norishige, but I knew from his manner that he would never confess, and so I cut off his head. He was two or three years past twenty and quite handsome. More and more suspicious, I searched under his armor and found a brocade bag strapped to his shoulder. The bag contained a tiny enshrined image of Kannon, and wrapped about the shrine was a letter in a woman's graceful hand.

The letter, according to "Confessions of Dōami," was as follows:

TO ZUSHO: *Seventh Month* 1554
To avenge my father you are to shoot off Norishige's nose, but you must not take his life. If you accomplish this for me, it will be an act of the greatest devotion.

For a moment, Terukatsu stood holding the scrap of paper in a daze on the dusty battlefield. The warrior lying there would be the "Zusho" to whom the letter was addressed. But the author? What woman asked the samurai Zusho "to shoot off Norishige's nose"? There was no signature, but from the sentence "If you accomplish this for me it will be an act of the greatest devotion," and from the way the address was written, small and at the bottom, Terukatsu judged that the letter had been sent to a subordinate by a high-ranking lady who wanted to conceal her name. Anyone other than Terukatsu reading the letter would have been at a loss to understand why the lady wanted Norishige's nose but not his life, and how that would "avenge my father"; indeed, it would have been hard even to take the letter seriously. But as Terukatsu stared at the mysterious tracings of the brush, he began to understand.

"Lady Kikyō . . ."

The thought sent shivers through Terukatsu's body, sweltering under his armor. Though he had been a retainer to the House of Tsukuma since the time of the late Ikkansai, he naturally was not allowed to enter the family's private residence and had never seen Lady Kikyō's face; he had heard rumors of her great beauty, but nothing concerning her character had reached him. He did not, therefore, recognize this feminine hand. Yet the man referred to as "father" by the woman who wrote the letter must be none other than Masataka, whose nose he had cut off. The meaning of the secret message had become clear to Terukatsu. Lady Kikyō must have been one of the very few family members aware that something vital had been missing from her dead father's face. Deeply chagrined, she wanted to avenge him by doing to the living face of the Tsukuma leader what had been done to her father's death face. Whether she married into the Tsukuma clan with that intention, or was moved to it after her marriage, it was, no doubt, her own idea, and not the wish of her brother Masahide. Had he felt that much bitterness over his father's unnatural death, he would never have agreed to a reconciliation with the Tsukuma clan, much less have allowed his sister to marry Norishige, whatever the shogunate might have said. And the means of revenge was too devious to have been devised by a man. Masahide would not have been so craven; he would have resorted to open, aboveboard means. Since the missive Zusho carried was in a woman's hand, and the revenge plot so very feminine in conception, Terukatsu concluded that Lady Kikyō had divulged to Zusho, a trusted samurai, the secret plan she had nurtured in her breast. Without a word to her family, she had resolved to avenge her father in the most cynical way.

These speculations lured Terukatsu's heart in an unexpected direction. His service to the Tsukuma House was, to be sure, a temporary expedient, not the consequence of a hereditary lord–vassal relationship; but he owed the family a debt of gratitude for his upbringing, and so, quite naturally, he had been no different from the other retainers in his feelings of esteem and affection for Norishige, and in his desire to serve faithfully. When this critical message came fortuitously into his possession, Terukatsu should have been overjoyed at having averted the calamity that threatened Norishige, and reported it to him at once. Such was his duty under the circumstances. Instead, his thoughts took an astonishing turn. The affinity for woman-heads that had slumbered so long in the recesses of his mind suddenly awakened and assumed a vivid shape. He envisioned that half-smile on the cheeks of the girl in the attic, and then transposed it to the face of the aristocratic lady who dwelt in the depths of the castle on Ojika Mountain. He sketched an image of the beautiful woman he had never seen: secluding herself in a room enclosed with gold screens that faintly reflected the light from the garden, leaning on an armrest in the shadow of her reed blinds, she would be gazing silently at the world outside with cold, beautiful eyes. The subtle smile that would play on her clear, pale cheeks as she pictured her husband Norishige, deprived of his nose, attracted Terukatsu far more strongly than that of the girl in the attic. That girl had been merely the daughter of someone called Ida of Suruga, but this was a lady of gentle birth, descended from the Middle Counselor of the Chrysanthemum Pavilion. The unconscious smile of Ida's daughter had been set off by a tinge of cruelty, nothing more, whereas the smile on this lady's elegant cheeks harbored a deep strain of mockery. It was the malevolent smile of a woman feigning virtue even as she quietly savored revenge. Terukatsu thought first of this lady, possessed of frightening malice, and then of her husband Norishige, mutilated by her desperate trick but still alive. When he juxtaposed their faces, one the embodiment of Beauty, the other of Ugliness, the wild joy that they inspired far surpassed anything he had felt in the attic. He had dreamed of the rapturous joy he would feel if he were a woman-head, one that had not lost consciousness, placed at the girl's knees and manipulated in her hands. Now one of the men he knew best would become a living "woman-head" and

bask in his wife's cold gaze. Soon—it was not impossible—
Terukatsu might witness the actual scene.

As you know, Japanese histories and biographies, particularly after the establishment of military rule in the Ka-
makura Period, have been exceedingly generous in relating
the words and deeds of heroes, but have had nothing to
say about the personalities of the women who bore these
heroes and who, in all likelihood, manipulated them behind
the scenes. Thus in the case of Lady Kikyō, too: from the
Genealogy of the House of Tsukuma and scattered entries
in contemporary military chronicles, we can establish her
lineage, the dates of her marriage and death, and that she
bore a son and a daughter to Norishige; but the only hint
that she conspired with Terukatsu to ruin Norishige comes
in a suggestive line or two of the *Tsukuma War Chronicles*,
and nothing at all can be learned from the official histories
about the circumstances behind the conspiracy, or about
what sort of woman she really was. A man who has masochistic sexual appetites, as the Lord of Musashi did, is apt
to construct fantasies in which his female partner conforms
to his own perverse specifications; and so the woman, in
most cases, is not at all the pitiless creature she is made out
to be. Concerning Lady Kikyō's mutilation of her husband,
we have Terukatsu's version in "Confessions of Dōami"
and the observations of the nun Myōkaku in "The Dream
of a Night," but the two accounts are so contradictory that
they often seem to describe different people. If we believe
the former, Lady Kikyō was innately sadistic; if the latter,
it would seem that her terrible resolve came only from a
desire to avenge her father's humiliation, and that normally
she was a gentlehearted woman. The latter is probably
closer to the truth; but perhaps, because the nun Myōkaku
had no firsthand knowledge of Lady Kikyō, she chose to

be discreet. Whatever the case may be, Terukatsu's singular appetites must have been stimulated by the cruelty of a wife who would mutilate her own husband and then take pleasure in gazing at his deformity as she attended him. From that moment, he became the lady's votary and secret ally and discarded his allegiance to Norishige like an old shoe.

Later I learned that Zusho was the son of Matoba Saemon, a Yakushiji retainer. His mother was Lady Kikyō's nurse, and so he and the lady were like brother and sister. He was a noted marksman. I believe that he severed his ties with his master at the time of the Tsukigata Castle insurrection and galloped from the capital to join Yokowa Buzen. It was he who had fired at Ikkansai the year before. Leaving his head on the battlefield, I concealed the Kannon shrine and the letter under my armor and returned to camp. No one learned of Lady Kikyō's treachery. Killing the man was the greatest mistake of my life, but from that moment my heart changed. I would be her ally and help her to realize her desire.

In other words, Terukatsu's morbid lust and Lady Kikyō's desire for revenge coincidentally sought satisfaction in the same object: to render Norishige noseless without killing him. Thus, for both of them it was inconvenient that Terukatsu had killed Zusho, the most important person for the realization of their objective. Unfortunately for Norishige, a comical episode was soon to follow.

In Which Tsukuma Norishige Acquires a Harelip, and the Toilets of High-Ranking Ladies Are Described

In the spring of 1555, about six months after the battle at Tsukigata Castle, Tsukuma Oribenoshō Norishige held a blossom-viewing party in the garden of the inner palace at

Ojika Castle. The cherry trees were in full bloom. He put up curtains and a carpet in the shade of the trees. There he drank sake and amused himself with poetry and music, accompanied by his wife and ladies-in-waiting. The party began in the morning and continued until a hazy moon hung in the evening sky. When lamps had been brought in and arranged on the carpet, Norishige, quite drunk by now, had a blind musician accompany him with a hand drum while he sang and danced a *kusemai*. As he neared the end of the dance—

> *The blossom's brocade sash*
> *Untied, but futilely*
> *The willow threads in disarray my heart*
> *Never can forget*
> *That hair in sleepy disarray*

—an arrow suddenly grazed Norishige's face, threatening to scatter his nose with the cherry blossoms, but it was low and caught him in the upper lip.

"Villain!"

Norishige was sure that he saw a dark figure spring from the branch of a cherry tree some forty feet away. Pressing a hand to his bleeding mouth, he shouted—or tried to shout, but for some reason his pronunciation was garbled. Frantically he tried to call out, "There! He went that way!" But he could only utter strange, inarticulate noises, quite without meaning, like the babblings of an infant. The arrow had split his upper lip and gums; the pain made it difficult for him to move his lips properly, and his breath escaped through the gaping wound. But at the time, with blood streaming from his face, he could not be sure whether he had been struck in the nose or in the mouth. When he realized that he could not understand his own words, his bewilderment was complete.

As men were rarely allowed to enter this part of the castle, it was the women in attendance who gave chase to the sniper. In the meantime, a number of samurai hurried to the scene and searched every corner of the spacious garden, but the sniper managed to hide somehow and was not to be found. No one could understand how this mysterious incident had occurred. The inner palace was in the center of the main citadel, and an intruder would have had to cross any number of defense posts to reach it. And though it was an Isle of Women, off limits to men, guards kept an alert watch day and night from strategic points all around. Someone who knew the way might follow the secret mountain path and approach the keep from the rear, but he would still find it difficult to infiltrate the inner garden. Not even samurai from the castle could reach it without passing two or three checkpoints. It was a wonder, then, that the sniper had stolen his way in, and, to compound the mystery, a thorough search of the garden turned up no trace of him. Everyone assumed that he could not have escaped to the outside and must be hiding somewhere in the compound. The search continued through the night, in the garden, in each room of the palace, in the attics and corridors and under the floors, but fruitlessly, to the increased apprehension of the people in the castle. The guards were reinforced and constant night patrols were ordered, but a month passed, and then two, without further incident, and the sniper's identity went unknown.

All the samurai rejoiced that their master's life was not in danger, but everyone who met him after the incident secretly pitied him. When the wound had healed enough for him to receive his men, it was apparent to all that he had acquired a harelip. It could not have been described as a serious injury. A slight irregularity in the contour of his lip would neither interfere with his daily activities nor prevent him from handling a sword on the battlefield like an ordinary man. Compared with a cripple or one who had lost an eye, he was scarcely handicapped at all, and so his men congratulated him on his good fortune; but none of them, when they bowed with feigned respect, looked directly at his face. To their great discomfort, they could not always make out what their master said. The situation improved somewhat as the wound continued to heal, but a triangular gap remained in the middle of his upper lip and two or three teeth were missing, with the result that certain sounds were indistinct. This was the extent of the physiological damage.

But one grows used to such things, and in time neither the person concerned nor those around him pay them the slightest attention. Norishige was dejected at first; but presently his retainers got so they could look at his face as if nothing had happened and learned to understand his speech. His handicap was taken for granted by everyone, and he forgot his initial embarrassment. Citing the example of Yamamoto Kansuke, the lame, squint-eyed, dwarfish strategist, some of his retainers assured him that physical defects only enhance one's dignity, and Norishige was gradually persuaded that this was indeed so. But to a dispassionate observer, or to one with a malicious turn of mind, nothing is so amusing as a comical situation that no one else finds humorous. The more the other retainers grew accustomed to them, the more Norishige's face and speech seemed comical to Terukatsu; and no matter how he tried to collect himself, he knew that he could not be loyal to the man when he looked at that triangular lip. On the contrary, the ugliness of Norishige's face intensified his devotion to Lady Kikyō. He longed to steal a look at the lady, preferably when she was alone with the harelip daimyo in their bedchamber. The lord of the pitiful face would utter sweet nothings in that peculiar voice, and his beloved wife Lady Kikyō would suppress a laugh, hide her sly malevolence, and smile coquettishly. This scene, doubtless repeated every night deep in the palace, was enacted in Terukatsu's daydreams whenever he came before Norishige. At times he thought he could see the noble lady's chalky face floating like a phantom in the shadowy alcove behind Norishige as he sat stiffly on his dais.

Terukatsu passed many happy days savoring the fantasies that Norishige's face inspired, but he too had no idea who had stolen into the garden and shot the disfiguring arrow. Probably you have assumed that it was Terukatsu himself, but apparently it was not. Under the circumstances it would be natural to suspect him, but "Confessions of Dōami" and "The Dream of a Night" speak of another culprit, as we shall see, and it seems most reasonable to accept their account. They are so outspoken about the darker aspects of the Lord of Musashi's secret life that it is unlikely they would cover for him and misrepresent the facts if he were guilty in this case. Besides, no communication had been established yet between him and Lady Kikyō. He might well have attempted some secret mischief, but it would certainly have failed if he were not in contact with the lady. When carried away by perverse passion, he turned into something completely unlike his usual self; but essentially he was a manly and noble warrior. At the time, he probably felt no more than an urge to do some mischief; surely his morbid tendencies had not developed far enough for him to stoop so low. Without any question, it was someone else's deed. The blossom-viewing incident had occurred just when Terukatsu was feeling the deepest regret for having killed Zusho and frustrated the lady's plan. Since he was not in attendance at the scene, he did not know the details; but he sensed immediately that the lady had refused to abandon her plans, and, furthermore, had found someone to play the role of a second Zusho. Of course he did not know how this man, or woman, had entered the inner garden and then escaped; but it was clear that everything had been carried out under the lady's aegis. And he realized that the arrow that had split Norishige's lip had been intended for his nose. Would the lady be satisfied to have given her husband a harelip? Or would the attacks continue until she had obliterated his nose? It was on this point that Terukatsu's interest inevitably came to rest.

One hot summer evening in the Sixth Month of the same year, Norishige was relaxing on the verandah with his wife, enjoying the breeze and drinking sake, when suddenly an arrow came flying from a dense grove in the garden. It was shot from the same direction and at the same angle to Norishige's face as before; but this time, Norishige heard it cut through the quiet night air. He averted his face and leaned back reflexively. Had he not done so, the protuberance above his harelip might have been flattened. Even so, he did not come off unscathed, for the arrow was faster than his dodge. As he pulled his torso back and twisted his neck to the left, the arrow grazed the right side of his face and swept away a protruding lump of flesh and cartilage—his right ear.

The ladies-in-waiting sprang into action, one group attending to Norishige and another dashing into the garden with lances. Nothing had occurred in the three months since the blossom-viewing party, and the search for the culprit had been given up as hopeless; vigilance had relaxed somewhat, but the guards instantly threw up a tight cordon, drawing on their experience in the previous attack. The sniper, however, must have soared into the sky or burrowed underground, for this time, too, he escaped detection.

The damage caused by Norishige's wound was as small, indeed, even slighter, than before. It was a heavy blow to his appearance, of course, to lose his right ear when he had already acquired a harelip, but this was preferable to losing his nose. It could be argued that losing an ear is even worse than gaining a harelip or going noseless, because it upsets the symmetry of the face; but this is something that each will have to decide for himself. The residents of Ojika Castle, far from considering such questions, were in a terrible state of anxiety and excitement. They concluded that the culprit was almost certainly the same person as before; but if the sniper had hidden all this time in the inner palace, then he or she had to be a member of the household. Consequently, the searches and investigations began with the palace orderlies and stewards (for though technically off limits to men, the palace employed some male servants), and worked up to the ladies-in-waiting; but suspicion fell most heavily on the concubines. Typically, a daimyo favored his concubines over his wife, but Norishige had married the woman he loved and kept two or three concubines only from habit and because it was expected of a feudal lord. The extent of his neglect of them can be seen in the fact that he had two children by his wife and none by his concubines. Previously he had gone to see them on a whim from time to time, but since his face had been visited by the unfortunate accident, he had rarely left his wife's side at night and had been loath even to be seen by the concubines. In the course of things, an especially jealous lady was singled out for close interrogation, but in the end there was no evidence against her and the investigation came to nothing.

Though the search was not abandoned completely, the prospects were not encouraging. The watches were carried out ever more rigorously and the number of guard posts

was increased, with a trusted retainer assigned each month
to supervise them. It was about two months later, in mid-
autumn, that Terukatsu was finally given his turn at the
guard posts. He had been waiting eagerly. Indeed, being
the only one who had sniffed out the secret he was better
suited than anyone else to this duty; but of course a desire
to serve Norishige by finding evidence of the plot was not
the reason for his eagerness. Since the guard posts were at
a far remove from Lady Kikyō's private chambers, there
was little hope of his establishing even indirect communication, let alone peeping at her; yet for one who adored
her from a distance, it was a comfort just to be a little closer
and to see the color of the tiles and walls of the palace in
which she lived. After assuming his new duties, Terukatsu
strolled around the outermost wall of the inner palace every
night directing the placement of lookouts, all the while
reveling in his usual fantasies as he pictured the strangely
contrasting couple in their bedroom. Even during the day,
he would lean against a sunny stone wall below the palace,
gaze at the clear autumn sky, and absently pursue the phantoms in his mind. At such times the battlefield hero became
a poet. It was the quietest, most secluded spot in the castle
grounds, the ideal place for a lovesick youth to pass the
time in conversation with his daydreams. As we have seen,
the castle of the Tsukuma clan was a mountain fortress
that exploited the natural stronghold of Mount Ojika. It
did not incorporate Western castle-building techniques,
as the later Azuchi Castle did, but was in pure medieval
style: the interior followed the dictates of topography and,
though spacious, was irregular in the extreme, with forests,
valleys, and brooks inside the walls. The inner palace was
situated on a hill that connected with a larger, gourd-
shaped hill, on which was built the outer palace. The narrow gourd neck linking the two hills was transversed by

a long gallery that led from the outer palace to the private rooms. A cedar door in the middle of the gallery marked the boundary between the sexes. This gallery was the only indoor route from the world of men to the world of women. The territory watched over by the guards encompassed the entire hill on which the inner palace stood, and so must have included a considerable area. The flat space at the top of the hill was enclosed by an earthen wall which, in turn, abutted on a sheer stone wall. The slope below the wall was left in its natural state, with weeds growing thick and high, a rocky precipice here and there, and an ominously dark, dense virgin forest. Someone venturing here might think he was lost in a trackless mountain wilderness.

One afternoon Terukatsu came as usual to his lonely spot at the base of the stone wall. As he sat absentmindedly on the root of a tree, his gaze strayed up the stone wall and over the towering earthen wall to the treetops of the luxuriant forest that overspread the inner garden, and, finally, to the roof that could be glimpsed between the treetops. "That is her palace," he said to himself. Close as he was, he had no way to declare his wish to be her loyal retainer and undertake whatever thankless task she might assign. The thought both filled him with chagrin and exacerbated his longing. Brimming with helpless yearning, his eyes might have lingered indefinitely on the stone wall and the roof, but all at once he noticed a place at the foot of the wall that was stripped of moss. At first he thought nothing of it; but, though the rest of the wall was covered with green, there were signs at this spot that someone had made scratches in the moss and then, to disguise them, had peeled off bits of the surrounding moss. Terukatsu stood up and tapped two or three times on the surface of the barest stone. It sounded as though there was a hollow space behind. He confirmed this by tapping on other rocks for comparison. Then he observed that the ground was scuffed and the weeds trampled, as if someone had moved the stone and then put it back. Finding a space just right for inserting his fingers, he tried joggling the stone. It slipped right out as he pulled. Terukatsu was fascinated. The stone had been easy to dislodge because it was hewn to less than half the thickness of its neighbors. A handle seven or eight inches long had been cut into the backside, so that the stone could be pulled back into place from inside the wall. With the stone out of the way, the hole in the wall was just large enough to admit a man's head and shoulders. Removing his longsword, Terukatsu squeezed through the opening, just as one does in the Buddhist purification rite known as "passing through the womb." Once inside, he had room to move around, and so he retrieved his sword, then grasped the handle and replaced the stone. He was plunged into darkness, but the tunnel, just large enough to crawl through, led him naturally uphill. At times the floor of the tunnel turned into a steep flight of stone steps. It seemed to him that he crept this way for an absurd length of time. How many yards, how many hundreds of yards it extended he could not gauge precisely, but finally the underground passage came to an end at the edge of a vertical shaft that intersected it at a right angle. He groped for a pebble which he dropped into the shaft. It was very deep, and Terukatsu knew roughly where he was.

At this point, I hope to be forgiven for raising a rather indelicate subject, the design of the toilets used by aristocratic ladies of the time. It is said that a famous Yoshiwara courtesan displayed her refinement by pretending to mistake a string of coins for a caterpillar; but ladies born into a daimyo family were not only ignorant of money, they never allowed anyone to see their excretory matter, nor did they ever see it themselves. Such delicacy was accomplished by digging under the toilet a deep shaft which was filled in for eternity when the lady died. Surely there is no more elegant method for disposing of feces. One is astonished by the luxury of Ni Yun-lin's toilet, contrived in such a way that solid objects falling into it would be instantly swallowed up by countless moth wings; but this does not match the gentility of the other method, which succeeds without allowing even the servants to see anything. Then there is the story of the beautiful Heian court lady who tantalized a suitor with a copy of her feces fashioned out of cloves. Discretion of this order was shared by all high-born ladies. In contrast, the modern flush toilet, while satisfying the requirements of cleanliness and hygiene, lays everything bare before your very eyes, and so, it must be said, is an ill-mannered, vulgar device, the designer of which must have forgotten that there is such a thing as decorum even when one is alone.

Such vertical shafts were reserved for aristocratic ladies and girls, however; and, as the little girl in the palace was only in her second year, this shaft could be used by just one person. In other words, Terukatsu now found himself deep in the earth directly beneath Lady Kikyō's toilet.

Book IV

⚜ ⚜ ⚜ ⚜ ⚜

In Which Lady Kikyō Meets Terukatsu and Conspires with Him

How incongruous it must have been for Terukatsu, destined to become the notorious Lord of Musashi, the majestic warrior of the portrait, to crouch like a mole in a tunnel under Lady Kikyō's toilet. No doubt he grimaced when he considered the compromising position he was in. However strong his admiration for the lady might have been, it would impair her dignity and reflect on his honor as a samurai if he tried to reach her by wriggling through this discourteous bypath. And suppose he accepted these handicaps. How could he intrude without alarming Lady Kikyō? If he caused her to cry out in surprise, or to faint, this unique opportunity would end in total failure. But Terukatsu was encouraged by his conjecture that the sniper, too, had used this underground passage. If so, then Lady Kikyō was used to having people leap from her toilet. She would not necessarily consider it an impertinence and, at the very least, she would hardly be so rash as to call for help just because a man had appeared unexpectedly. This realization quickly refreshed his curiosity and sense of adventure.

Terukatsu waited some time for the noble lady to reign overhead; but he could not stay at the edge of the hole very long, and presently had to withdraw disappointed. At about the same time on each of the next three days, he stole to the base of the wall, entered the underground passage, and waited patiently for about an hour at the brink of the vertical shaft. His persistent efforts, so reminiscent of the hell tour at Zenkō Temple, were finally rewarded on the afternoon of the third day, when soft footsteps sounded on the floor above and a faint ray of light penetrated the darkness in the passage. He made a slight noise to draw her attention.

"Your Ladyship," he called, as gently and softly as he could. "May it please you, I have something to say. Might I be admitted to your presence?"

The rustle of silk stopped suddenly. He guessed that she was standing still and listening beside the black-lacquered rim from which his voice had come. Terukatsu drew Zusho's secret note from his breast.

"It concerns this letter," he said, holding the paper up where she could see it. "You have nothing to fear from me. Please admit me."

His plan had the desired effect. Softly she replied, "You may come up."

The shaft, which had often been used for this purpose, was provided with suitable footholds, so that a person might climb unsoiled and with the least possible strain into the room; and so Terukatsu was able to rise smartly through the black-lacquered rim and prostrate himself before her without resorting to postures that might impair his honor, and without compromising the lady's dignity. The scene was much like that on the stage in *The Thousand Cherry Trees*, where the fox, disguised as Tadanobu, appears from beneath a palace corridor and bows to Lady Shizuka. In fact, even though it was a toilet, the room (which was enclosed by walls and paneled double doors) was spacious enough that a lady, looking like a huge flower in her bulky robes, could move freely about. It was floored completely with straw mats and gave the impression of silent expanse

that one expects of a palace room. Overawed, Terukatsu
pressed his forehead to the matted floor. The faint bouquet
of fine incense in the air around him inspired still greater
awe, and he tucked his head in against his chest. The lady's
robes may have been imbued with the aroma of some rare
incense; or perhaps it was the scent of smoldering aloes, for,
though he could not see it, there was a small window near
Terukatsu's head, and on the shelf in front of the window
lay a celadon incense burner.

"Who are you?"

"I am Terukatsu, Vice-Governor of Kawachi, eldest son
of Kiryū Terukuni, Lord of Musashi."

When he spoke, the thick fabric in her robes, the skirts
of which fanned out and rose in heavy swells two or three
feet from his face, rustled crisply as the lady, suppressing
her astonishment, took a step back.

"You say you are Terukatsu?"

"Yes, Your Ladyship."

"Lift your face."

The young samurai raised his head respectfully and
gazed for the first time on the woman who had been the
object of his longings. In the best of circumstances, one
naturally cannot stare in the face of an eminent person;
much less could this inexperienced youth do so when he
found himself face to face with the woman he had adored
from a distance. Sunlight never penetrated to the dark
rooms at the back of a palace, and the toilet room was illuminated only by the weak light of a fall afternoon reflected
against the paper window. The lady's face, as he searched
it out in the twilight dimness, was probably as hazy as the
phantom he had sketched in his mind. For the rest, he would
have had to imagine how graceful and refined a lady she
was on the basis of her dimly white face. All he could make
out clearly was the pattern embroidered on her robes in

gold thread and leaf, which show best in dark places. Seeing that she stood with one hand prudently on the handle of her dagger, he bowed his head again reverently.

"You really are Terukatsu," she said, half to herself. Terukatsu had never seen her before, but she had often seen him. Upper-class women of the time rode in palanquins when they went outdoors, or were heavily veiled, and indoors they always concealed themselves behind curtains and reed blinds. Hence there was no danger of the male retainers seeing her face, but she was free to look at theirs.

At seasonal banquets, theatrical performances, tournaments, recitals, and the like, Lady Kikyō must often have noted the youth's promising mien and physique among the ranks of retainers. "That is Terukatsu, who has such a reputation for bravery," her attendants would have whispered as she peered through her reed blinds. Terukatsu had anticipated as much, but he felt supremely honored by her words. Knowing that she remembered him intensified his deep sense of gratitude at this happy first meeting.

"May it please you, I have come as your ally." Catching her unspoken question, he was anxious first of all to win her trust. In an eager and passionate tone, he continued.

"Your ally—I am your ally. Please entrust me with the assignment in this letter, the duties of Matoba Zusho."

When he mentioned Matoba Zusho, a trembling "Oh!" escaped her lips, but she quickly regained her composure.

"Show me the letter," she said as softly as she could. Terukatsu held it up to her as if he were presenting a formal petition. Turning the note to the feeble light from the window, she examined it briefly and put in in her breast.

"Where did you get this?"

"It was I who killed Matoba Zusho in the fall of last year at the battle of Tsukigata Castle. I thought that he was trying to kill my lord with a gun. After taking his head, I searched him and found the letter inside a charm bag. The forces were engaged in a fierce battle at the time, and no one else knows of this."

"And why . . . ," she began, but not knowing what to think, she broke off and stared at Terukatsu for a moment. He would be a formidable enemy, yet here he was groveling at her feet and begging to be accepted as an ally. Nothing could be more fortunate; but she could not understand what motivated the youth to forget his obligations to the House of Tsukuma and devote himself to her, with whom he had no ties whatsoever. Yet she could hardly doubt his goodwill when she considered that the secret message had never been brought out in the open. It was an age when people resorted to the most desperate schemes to ensnare their enemies, and she would be cautious; but, then, if he intended to expose her crime, why should he be so indiscreet as to surrender this incontrovertible evidence to her? He let her do as she pleased with the note and appeared to be quite overcome with awe; such was not the attitude of someone plotting against her.

"Please, look at this." Realizing that she was not about to relax her vigilance, Terukatsu took a small brocade pouch from his breast and lifted it reverently to his head.

"This is a Kannon shrine. Zusho carried it with the letter under his armor. Since then I have always kept it with me as a sign that I, inadequate as I am, will carry out his mission." In his enthusiasm, he opened the pouch as he spoke and was about to remove the shrine.

"Here!" To remind him that they were in an unclean place, her eyes rebuked him and she signaled against doing anything sacrilegious; but she must have been moved by his ardor.

"And why do you wish to be my ally?" She spoke sternly, but with a touch of tenderness.

"Your Ladyship, I have something else to give you." Without answering her question, he reached into his breast again, withdrew a gold-embroidered pouch containing a small jar, and held it out respectfully to the lady.

"Inside this pouch is a memento of your father, Lord Masataka. Please accept it."

"What? A memento of my father?" she asked, as if she could not trust her ears.

"Yes, Your Ladyship," Terukatsu replied immediately. Holding the pouch high in both hands, he bowed his head deeply. "I believe that something precious was missing, most deplorably, from Lord Masataka's body."

"Do you mean to say that it's inside this pouch?"

"Yes, Your Ladyship."

Standing before Terukatsu in robes three times bulkier than his, the lady swayed gracefully like a peony that droops and falls; and then there was a great rustle of silk, like the sound of wind in the pines on a mountain crest. When she heard Terukatsu's reply, she had pressed her hands together reverently before the object he was holding and had fallen to her knees.

"Terukatsu," she began, after a moment of silence. Abandoning her former reserve, she now spoke in the most feminine way. "Where did you get this memento of Father?"

"When Lord Masataka laid siege to this castle, he pressed the attack to the third, and then to the second citadel. The castle was about to fall when the late master Ikkansai summoned a spy secretly and commanded him to strike Lord Masataka during the night. No one but I heard him."

"Then it was just as I thought." She heaved a sigh.

Suddenly agitated, she leaned forward. "You say that only you heard him?"

"That is correct. I was twelve years old at the time. As

I passed through a corridor near the late master's study, I heard him whisper, 'If you don't have time to take his head, just the nose will do.' I knew it was wrong of me, but his words were so strange, I stopped. Then I heard him say, 'All right? Just the nose, if necessary. Even if you don't kill him, that fop will be sure to pull back his forces and run if he loses his nose.' And then he laughed quietly, 'ha, ha.' The castle might have fallen at any moment, and perhaps he had no choice; but sending a spy to take the enemy general's head as he slept, let alone instructing him to cut off the general's nose, did not sound like the late master we all knew. He must have been ashamed to have anyone hear of it, for as soon as the plan had been executed and the spy had returned to the castle, Lord Ikkansai killed him and discarded his body without telling anyone the reason. This memento was in the man's breast."

As he spoke, Terukatsu saw drops of dew gather on the lady's long eyelashes, now only a foot or two from him, and roll down her smooth, white cheeks. With this pitiable beauty before him, he gradually regained the composure to exercise his foresight and eloquence fully. For two or three days he had toiled over the outlines of a story that would convince her, and even he was impressed by the plausible sequence of his explanation.

"Though I was just a child, I was indignant when I overheard the master's secret plan. It was not the sort of conduct I expected from a samurai. On the other hand, I pitied the spy who had been killed, and the next day, I think it was, I went to a valley in the hills behind the keep to see his body. I finally found him among the piles of corpses. He might be carrying some proof of his deed, I thought, and so I searched his clothes. This memento is what I found. Probably the master decided it was useless and discarded it with the body. But I thought it wrong to handle a memento of the general without due respect, even if he were the enemy. It was my good fortune as a samurai that, through some wonderful fate, this came into my hands. Whatever the master might have had in mind, I for my part had to do what a samurai must do, and so I took it back to my quarters and preserved it in red ink. I have guarded it until now in the hope that someday there would be an opportunity to return it to the Yakushiji family. And so, Your Ladyship, that is how I came to have it."

"You are too kind, Terukatsu." With unfeigned gratitude, the lady put her hands on the floor of the toilet room and, with her rich black hair trailing over her noble face, bowed to the youth.

"I heard of your outstanding courage, but I never thought that such a young man could be so considerate. You did well to understand our position. You can imagine, then, how I feel."

"Yes, Your Ladyship. Most humbly, I can imagine."

"Born into a samurai house, I know that I might lose members of my family at any time, and, though I am just a woman, I am reconciled to it. If Father had died on the battlefield, I could have accepted his loss with resignation; but as his daughter, how could I ever forget the way he was killed—like the act of a sneak thief!—and the unspeakable humiliation he suffered? You know I could not. They told me he had died of illness, and I believed them. But when my mother and brother wouldn't allow me to see his face, I secretly pleaded with my nurse. Finally she had had enough of my pestering and gave in. 'All right, I'll let you see him,' she said. 'But your father did not pass on from illness. He will look very different, and you must not be alarmed.' Repeating this warning again and again, she secretly took me to see him. Why, you felt uncomfortable just hearing about it, though you are not related to him.

How bitter it was for me! My nurse took me in the middle of the night, and we were alone inside the reed blinds of the audience room where he lay in state. I saw poor Father's face under the light that my nurse held out for me. I was struck speechless. I could only press my face to her breast, my body trembling." Won over by Terukatsu's sympathy and devotion, the lady began to pour out her innermost feelings.

Her disclosures go on and on, but probably she did not make them all at their first meeting. It seems likely that they met in the same place at a regular time for the next two or three days, and that her story emerged little by little as they talked. According to the account in "Confessions of Dōami," there was an antechamber between the toilet room and the corridor, with thick cedar doors installed at each partition, so that a conversation in the room could not be heard outside. Of course an attendant stood by in the antechamber or the corridor beyond; and it was always Matoba Zusho's younger sister Haru who accompanied the lady to the toilet. You will recall that the lady's nurse was the mother of Matoba Zusho; when she married into the Tsukuma family, the lady brought her nurse and Haru with her.

As the story progresses, you will come to recognize a certain characteristic of the Lord of Musashi: however excited and engrossed he may appear to be in his peculiar lust, an instinct for self-preservation is always at work in the depths of his consciousness; and, moreover, continually led on by good luck, he sometimes uses even his weakness as a means of destroying his enemies. Masochistic pleasure is, after all, a form of pleasure, and so it clearly involves an element of self-interest; but there is always a danger that someone with this proclivity will go too far and be ruined. Yet the Lord of Musashi, even as he pursued his unique secret pleasure, was able to make steady inroads into the lands around him and expand his domain. At times, he would become too engrossed and be lured to the brink of disaster, but he never forgot to draw himself up short of the last step. The process by which he ingratiated himself to Lady Kikyō with an eloquent fabric of facts and lies is an illustration of this characteristic. It seems highly doubtful that the object he presented to her as "a memento of Lord Masataka" at their first meeting was actually a relic of Yakushiji Danjō Masataka at all. Even if the twelve-year-old Hōshimaru did retrieve Masataka's nose, he could not have anticipated what was occurring now, and so it is inconceivable that he would have preserved that scrap of flesh for six years. Perhaps the shrewd Terukatsu followed the example of Mongaku, the twelfth-century monk, who picked up a random skull and presented it to Yoritomo as the skull of his father Yoshitomo. Terukatsu probably cut a nose from one of the corpses that lay scattered nearby and used it as a tool to excite Lady Kikyō's hostility. When it comes to a skull, there is little difference between a nobody and a Yoshitomo; in the same way, no one could tell whether a piece of nose had come from a general or a private. In fact, since he had preserved it in red ink, it need not have been a nose at all: any soft lump of roughly the same shape would have sufficed. But it would be indelicate to speculate any further on what the object in the jar might have been. Suffice it to say that even a man of Yoritomo's stature was taken in when presented with a "memento" of his father; it is only human nature, and so it is no wonder that Lady Kikyō fell under a spell when she saw the mysterious gold-brocade bag.

"Confessions of Dōami" and "The Dream of a Night" differ in their views of Lady Kikyō, as I have said. But concerning her motives for scheming to mutilate her husband, the account in "The Dream of a Night" seems natural and penetrating. According to it, after she was taken by her nurse to see Masataka, his noseless face flashed before her eyes night after night and she was tormented by a cruel, obsessive vision of her father not quite dead in the world beyond. In other words, she believed that her slain father was drifting in space, unable to realize his desire for an easy passage into eternity because he had lost his nose. For her, this was a source of nearly unbearable grief. After his tragic death he should at least have been reborn in the Western Pure Land. But far from it; he still felt a lingering attachment to this world, because he had left something precious behind, and so could not rest in peace. The thought of her poor father, not only murdered but forced to endure this torment, gave her no respite. Every night in her dreams he appeared beside her pillow, pressing a hand to the middle of his face. She could hear him cry over and over, "I want my nose . . . please give back my nose." In short, she would not be able to sleep until she somehow found her father's nose and erased that horrible death face from her memory. "I blamed my nurse," she told Teru-katsu. "No matter how much I pestered her, she should never have let me see him when my mother and brother had done their best to prevent it. I would have been spared all this suffering." Indeed, it was rash of the nurse to let a girl of thirteen see such a thing, and the lady's grievance is both reasonable and touching. But she had seen him, there was no changing that, and so she would find his nose for him; yet that was an impossible assignment. Then the re-conciliation between the Yakushiji and Tsukuma clans, and her marriage to Norishige, unexpectedly presented her with the opportunity to comfort her father's spirit and ease her own distress.

Her brother Masahide had urged the match on her, declaring, "Father died of illness, as you know, and so there is no reason to bear grudges against the Tsukuma family. Let's have no misunderstanding about that." Given the position of women at the time, she had no right to oppose a political marriage arranged by the head of her family, particularly in view of the shogunate's advocacy; and so, for the sake of her family and the country, she could only sacrifice herself and submit blindly to the decisions handed down from above. Nevertheless, she thought that her brother lacked spirit in showing so little resentment over their father's death. Masahide was inclined to settle things amicably, for, after all, no one was sure who had killed Masataka and a public disclosure of the matter would hardly bring honor to their father's memory; but she had no faith in her brother's judgment. In fact, Masahide was even more fainthearted and effete than his father Masataka had been; and it was not long before a senior retainer named Baba seized his territory; Masahide lived on in disgrace after losing his clan and his domain, and wandered aimlessly around the country. Though Lady Kikyō pretended to know nothing about her father's death, she had her own ideas about it, quite different from her brother's. She was certain from the moment she saw her father's death face that he had lost his life in an enemy subterfuge. He had been killed, after all, in camp during a war, and the fact that the killer took his nose instead of his head proclaimed more eloquently than anything else that it was the work of an enemy agent. To regard it as the act of a robber or the consequence of some personal grudge was nothing more than a cowardly refusal to face the facts. She was sure that she was right, but when she realized that the rest of the clan, her mother and brother and the senior retainers, were not taking it so seriously, she thought that her father would never be able to rest in peace, and her grief intensified. For some time she had agonized over ways to divert her mind from this grief when suddenly it occurred to her to take advantage of her marriage into the Tsukuma clan and inflict upon Ikkansai and his son the same fate that had been inflicted upon her father.

She said that the sight of satisfactory noses on the faces of her father-in-law Ikkansai and her husband Norishige filled her with pity for her father. It probably made her angry to see a nose on anyone's face. The very fact that she had a nose herself must have pricked her conscience. Probably she thought that her father's misery could be relieved completely only if everyone in the world lost their noses. She was a bride of fifteen at the time, and neither old enough nor experienced enough to aspire after anything as ambitious as the destruction of the Tsukuma clan; and so the plan she came up with was exceedingly simple and girlish. In short, she was obsessed with the notion that her father's ghost would forget his anger, and her own grief would be assuaged, if she rendered her father-in-law or her husband noseless in place of all the people of the world. Consequently, her immediate target was their noses, not their lives. If by accident her victim lost his life along with his nose, so be it; but she would prefer to let him live for a time without his nose so that she could confirm his misery thoroughly with her own eyes and expose him to public ridicule. This is the basis for the view, expressed in "Confessions of Dōami," that she was innately sadistic. But according to "The Dream of a Night," she made the following confession to Terukatsu:

> Through her tears, Lady Kikyō said, "Is there anyone in the world so unfortunate as I? Though I am the daughter of his enemy, he is my husband and I do not hate him. What bond from a former life has caused me to plan this terrible revenge? I am certain to be reborn in hell anyway,

for I have heard that women are sinful creatures. But may the gods and buddhas be my witness, this revenge goes against my heart. It was inspired by that delusion about my father that lurks in my breast and whispers in my ear."

Only by fixing Ikkansai's or Norishige's noseless face clearly in her eyes until she was thoroughly satisfied, and not simply by killing them, would she be able to exorcise the ghastly nightmare that menaced her sleep every night. Her conduct after the fall of the Tsukuma clan makes it clear that she was not the sort of woman who would enjoy maiming her husband for no reason. She said herself that, "though the daughter of his enemy, I do not hate him," and it seems to be true that, deep in her heart, she loved and pitied the husband she mutilated. Her life, then, can be viewed as an unending struggle to erase the memory of her father's death face, to which end she sacrificed her husband, her children, and herself.

The first person to learn of Lady Kikyō's plan was her nurse, Matoba Saemon's wife, whose name was Kaede. No doubt Kaede was startled when the lady revealed her design, but she had been responsible for showing the death face to her in the first place and could not protest this new development too sharply. With time, she came to sympathize with her mistress and was drawn into the plot. Apparently her husband, Matoba Saemon, was not implicated; he had already died of natural causes by the time of Lady Kikyō's wedding. And so the widow Kaede, taking along her daughter Haru, went into service at Mount Ojika as the bride's maidservant, then gradually prevailed upon her children to join the conspiracy. The details are not known, but it is certain that Kaede and her daughter Haru, on the inside, and her son Matoba Zusho on the outside, conspired together to assist in Lady Kikyō's revenge. First Zusho went after Ikkansai's nose, and then, when that failed, after

Norishige's at the battle of Tsukigata Castle, where, finally, he was cut down by Terukatsu without realizing either goal. Who gave Norishige his harelip in the castle garden, and who shot off his ear? "Confessions of Dōami" and "The Dream of a Night" record that Zusho had a younger brother named Matoba Daisuke, who followed in his footsteps. With the connivance of his mother Kaede, Daisuke and an excavator who specialized in digging moats and trenches were carried into the palace inside a great trunk. It is not clear what became of them. We may assume that the excavator, after finishing the tunnel that Terukatsu discovered, was killed, thrown to the bottom of the shaft, and absorbed into the earth forever with the lady's excrement. What happened to Daisuke? Because of the strict surveillance after the incident at the blossom-viewing party, it would have been impossible for him to hide in the trunk again and escape without attracting attention. On the contrary, we are told that from the first incident to the second, during the four months that elapsed between splitting Norishige's lip and divesting him of an ear, Daisuke lay doubled up inside a cavelike cavity that had been specially dug near the top of the shaft. Never taking a step into the outside world, he subsisted there on rice balls provided by the lady and his mother. From ancient times there have been numerous examples of men who sacrificed themselves for the sake of their masters, their parents, or their brothers; but there cannot have been many who endured the hardships suffered by Daisuke, secluded for four months beneath a toilet. The reader must not confuse Daisuke's behavior with the shameful conduct of a pervert or sex maniac. He was motivated by uncomplicated loyalty and filial piety. And probably, when this faithful, courageous youth realized that he had fulfilled his mission as far as he was able, he fell nobly on his sword, cast his body into the same darkness that had received the excavator, and literally sank into his grave. Since Terukatsu did not meet him when he traversed the tunnel, Daisuke must already have taken his life.

But what did Lady Kikyō make of Terukatsu, this eccentric young warrior who was offering to serve in Daisuke's stead? Samurai did not share the Western concept of chivalry, according to which a man might venerate an aristocratic woman and consider it an honor to give his life for her. And so, while it may have been natural for Lady Kikyō to plot revenge against her father-in-law and husband, there was no reason for Terukatsu to join in. That his sympathy for her father and indignation over Ikkansai's contemptible trick—so unworthy of a samurai—led him to preserve the nose and deliver it to her might be credited to kindness and generosity. This much she could accept with gratitude. But his offer to assist in her unfinished revenge clearly went beyond the bounds of simple generosity or kindness. Lady Kikyō could not have known that he was motivated by the perverted desires that lurked in his breast; she must have been persuaded by some other consideration; that he had, for example, reasons of his own to bear a grudge against the Tsukuma clan, or that he felt so obligated to her that he would turn his back on the debt of gratitude he owed the clan. This line of thought leads to the conclusion that she must not have taken him into her confidence immediately, that even though she was momentarily won over by his sympathy when he showed her the fraudulent "memento" of her father, a lengthy process must have led to her decision to entrust him with something as important as her revenge. The *Tsukuma War Chronicles* hint at a secret liaison between Lady Kikyō and Terukatsu and imply that their love developed into a conspiracy; but Terukatsu was not the sort of man to make a false show of affection in order to win a lady's trust, nor is there any reason to suppose that he was particularly skilled in the art of seduction. Probably it is true that there was a liaison, but it seems likely that it developed later, when the two had gradually become intimate in the course of discussing the destruction of the Tsukuma clan. In other words, the conspiracy came first, then the physical relationship; and we may assume that it was not consummated frequently.

Most probably, Lady Kikyō concluded that Terukatsu's excessively generous offer was motivated by designs on the Tsukuma domain. Norishige was a man of mediocre capabilities; for Terukatsu, who was not a hereditary vassal, to embrace such an ambition would only be in character for a hero of that age of civil wars, and it would not have been surprising if he had sought to exploit the lady's vindictiveness to further his ambition. She must have realized that her husband would be hard put to hold his domain and cope with the turbulent times. She probably decided that the wisest course, for the sake of the continuity of the Tsukuma clan, was to endorse Terukatsu's designs, to use him to accomplish her revenge even as he used her, and, by appealing to Terukatsu's sympathy, to provide for the safety of her two children after Norishige's death. It is not clear how openly she and Terukatsu discussed their mutual interests; but she probably interpreted his desire to be her "ally" in this light, while he, concealing his secret motives, let her believe what she would; and so they reached a tacit understanding. If this is true, then it was Terukatsu's ambition that led Lady Kikyō to plot the overthrow of the Tsukuma clan, for originally she would have been satisfied simply to cut off Norishige's nose; and conversely, after Terukatsu had satisfied his peculiar sexual desire, his feigned ambition grew into something true. Before he realized it, his self-interest, shrewdness, and courage were coolly at work to seize the opportunity to crush the House of Tsukuma.

In Which Norishige Loses His Nose, and Concerning the "Village of Falling Blossoms" Poem from Genji

Unaware that a secret agreement had been reached between his beloved wife and a retainer, Norishige continued his nightly visits to the lady's bedchamber, where he would mumble unintelligible blandishments through his harelip. Pampered and optimistic as he was, he apparently could not help feeling dejected over his split lip and severed ear, for the *Tsukuma War Chronicles* record that "feeling unwell, he was prone from that time on to keep to his chambers." The more prone he was to stay in, however, the more he was at his wife's side. In the presence of retainers and ladies-in-waiting he was self-conscious about his face and naturally fell into a dark humor; but when he entered the secret room, dimly illuminated by the soft glow of a lamp, and saw the lady's alluring smile, he was able to forget the missing ear and triangular lip in his euphoria. As men of his sort are temperamentally unsuited to be warlords anyway, he was more comfortable leaving the administration of the manor to the senior vassals, and so he retired to the inner palace, using his wounds as an excuse. He may have looked melancholy, but perhaps he did not take his misfortunes so hard after all.

And so the Eighth Month passed. Normally the Ninth Month was the occasion for a moon-viewing party, the Chrysanthemum Festival, and foliage viewing, but this year the manor refrained from holding elaborate entertainments, public or private, because of the lord's indisposition, and the ceremonies were observed in their simplest forms. In any case, late fall on Mount Ojika was a deeply affecting time, with the sound of fallen leaves and the blasts of wind that brought drenching autumn showers. A hush fell over the inner palace; at night the garden grasses rustled ominously and from time to time, in the distance, the cry of a deer or fox echoed in the valley. Norishige had once been fond of assembling the young ladies-in-waiting to dance and play the koto, and he might have done so now to brighten his spirits; but lately the best he could do was to sit quietly with his wife, exchanging cups of sake, and he avoided festive amusements entirely. In part this was because of his bitter experience at the blossom-viewing party that spring; but there was another reason, too. Proud of his voice, he had always been ready to sing a ballad, but now, with his pronunciation impaired and his breath whistling through his lips, a beautiful voice did him no good. Unable to sing himself, he was jealous and chagrined when anyone else sang, and so lost interest in holding concerts.

It was an evening toward the middle of the Ninth Month. An autumn rain had begun to fall late in the afternoon and continued into the night as a gentle drizzle soaked quietly into the earth; the sound of drops running along the eaves was enough to lure a person into melancholy reveries. Norishige had been in his wife's room since early evening, affectionately exchanging cups of sake with her as Oharu served. Sipping wine with a lover while listening to the sound of a lonely rain is a pleasant thing for anyone, but this evening Norishige had consumed far more than usual and was in exceptionally good spirits. Now and then he would hand the cup to his wife and say, "Here, won't you drink a little more?" As he grinned bashfully at her profile, his smiling eyes revealed a good-natured man with a bit of the spoiled child in him. In his pronunciation, though, the words came out something like "Here, won' you hrink a li'l more?" but this no longer bothered him. Previously he had, it is true, been in the habit of speaking majestically on formal occasions to maintain his dignity as a daimyo; but since acquiring a harelip he had come to speak timidly, and so, even now, when he was completely at ease, his voice could sometimes be as faint as the hum of a mosquito. Probably the reason that he grew bashful when he looked at his wife's face was that, deep in his heart, he was embarrassed to be so hopelessly in love with her; but another reason may have been that he was conscious of being a "cripple," and this awareness was reflected in his actions. In any case, before his disfigurement, Norishige had been a swaggering, devil-may-care sort, with nothing timorous about him.

As she sipped her cup of sake, Lady Kikyō seemed to be listening to the rain in the garden.

"Listen to that," she said with a frown, "it still seems to be raining."

"So it is, but it's a gentle, fleasant rain, isn't it."

"Yes, now that you mention it, this evening truly feels like autumn. But I get lonely and depressed on evenings like this."

"For some reason the sake tastes esfecially good tonight. The sound of the rain is relaxing."

"I'm glad. Nothing makes me so happy as to see you in a good mood."

"Why hon't you write a foem on the mood of this autumn evening?" This sudden request was out of character for Norishige, but recently he had begun to take up odd pastimes to relieve his boredom and had been learning the art of poetry from his wife. She naturally was proficient in Japanese poetry and other courtly accomplishments, since her mother was the daughter of a courtier and she herself had been reared in the capital. With her help, Norishige had learned to string thirty-one syllables into something resembling a poem, and he would cry "Why hon't you write a foem" if anyone so much as dropped a chopstick.

The lady seemed to have anticipated this, and asked Oharu to bring paper and a writing box. The ink gave off a faint aroma as Oharu ground it. Holding a strip of heavy paper in one hand, the lady moved closer to the lamp and quickly traced a poem in beautiful calligraphy. If truth be told, Norishige was not interested in the quality of the poems. He loved to see his wife's expression when she leaned forward in the lamplight, lost in thought as she sorted out the phrases that came silently to her lips; for it seemed to him that she was at her most beautiful and noble when she was preoccupied this way. As he gazed fondly at her sculpturesque nose and lips vividly silhouetted in the lamplight, he would say to himself, "I've known many women, but a well-bred lady is something special," and sigh in admiration, or break into a grin as if a surge of joy had welled up inside him. Tonight in particular the flush on Lady Kikyō's cheeks, normally as white as her formal paper, added an indescribable voluptuousness to her classic, taut features. If Terukatsu had peeped in upon this scene, what sort of impression would it have made on him? In the center of the chilly, broad, high-ceilinged room stood a folding screen; the flame of a single lamp warded off the darkness of the night that pressed in from every side, and inside that circle of light, a drop of oil on a pool of water, sat three indistinct figures. Silently the lady moved her brush across the paper; her attendant quietly ground the ink; and now and then the master, basking in joy, licked the rim of his sake cup. Holding up the paper that his wife showed him, he read out her poem; but his whispery voice was swallowed up in the dark corners of the room, and it was impossible to make out what he said. The shadow of his head, with his hair tied back in the shape of a tea whisk and one ear missing, was cast large on the surface of the folding screen. In this light his harelip gaped like a cavern and filled the room with a ghastly aura, while even Lady Kikyō's elfin beauty was somehow ominous, as though of another world. And outdoors the wind-driven rain beat down portentously in the rapidly deepening night. The effect of this scene would surely have been no less extraordinary than that of heads being dressed in the attic.

After Lady Kikyō presented two or three poems, Norishige managed with some difficulty to produce one of his own, demonstrating the progress he had made. As they praised each other's skill, the evening's diversions came to an elegant conclusion. It was past ten o'clock when they retired to bed. For some time, Norishige caressed his wife, as he did every night; but now he felt the effects of drinking with nothing to eat but poetry, and his importuning and fawning grew more uninhibited as he abandoned himself to waves of ecstasy. In the end, he always fell asleep as if his body and soul had dissolved, but he would wake up several hours later and go to urinate. Tonight, too, he rose at about midnight, taking care not to disturb his wife, and went quietly to the antechamber, where Oharu was in attendance. She lit a hand lamp and led him into the passageway. His toilet was in the opposite direction from the lady's, about thirty feet down a long passage, then a turn to the left and a turn to the right, which led to a matted corridor ten or fifteen feet long. This was the darkest spot of all, with a wall on one side and wood sliding doors facing the garden on the other. When Norishige had tottered this far, still drowsy and intoxicated with sake and the other pleasure, he could hear the steady fall of rain against the planks of the verandah just beyond the doors.

"Hasn't stoffed yet, still hrizzling," he muttered to himself, as if he were talking in his sleep.

"Yes, sir, it is a depressing rain," said Oharu. She stopped in her tracks. "Be careful, My Lord. Please watch your step." She turned the light toward his unsteady feet. Just then, in the blackness obliterating everything behind her, there was a gust of wind, like the flutter of a wing, and with a gasp she dropped the lamp.

"Who's there?" cried Norishige. He thought he saw a black shape move in the darkness. A man? A monster? A hallucination? Wrapped in darkness now—the lamp had gone out as it fell—he could not tell if the image lingering in his retinas was that of something real or a nightmare conjured by his bleary, drowsy eyes. It was odd that Oharu had said nothing more.

"Haru! What haffen?" he called into the darkness. "What haffen? Is somebohy there?"

"M-M-My Lord! . . . Quickly . . . quickly . . ." It was certainly Oharu's voice, but it sounded as though her mouth were covered and she were being strangled. Mustering all her strength, she was calling out with her last breath. "Quickly, My Lord, r-r-run quickly!" Her words broke off; she groaned and fell to the floor with a thud. Holding his breath, Norishige inched to one side of the corridor and, spread out like a spider, pressed his back flat against the wall; but the intruder came right after him, wrapped a powerful arm around his neck, and rammed him against the wall with terrifying force. Feeling his body being pressed as flat as a cracker, Norishige tried several times to call out "Villain!" but the more he struggled, the deeper his opponent's arm cut into his neck. Slowly suffocating, he thought, "I'm lost, I'll be killed," as his mind started to go numb. Just then he felt the palm of his attacker's hand stroking his face. He resigned himself to being stabbed at the base of his throat with a dagger, but his assailant, still gripping his neck with one arm, continued to run the other hand all over his face, as if he were licking him with his tongue. After confirming that one ear was missing, the hand moved to the harelip and thoroughly explored the nose from base to tip, bridge and nostrils. Gradually losing consciousness, Norishige found this outrageous in the extreme. The man was making sport of him, he thought. He wanted to shout, "Insolent! What are you hoing!" But before he could, there was a dull crunch and he knew his nose was leaving his face. The attacker had loosened his grip slightly, permitting Norishige to breathe more easily; and at the same time, like a surgeon removing an excrescence with a scalpel, had cut systematically from the base, leaving behind no trace of anything resembling a nose.

When he finally regained consciousness, Norishige was like a man coming out of anesthesia after surgery. He remembered what had happened up to the time his nose was cut off but had no recollection of anything after. No doubt his attacker had either knocked him out when he finished the "surgery" or had tightened his grip on the neck again. Norishige had lost consciousness and, when he came to, he had already been carried to his wife's room and was lying on the bed. Because she had fallen before he had, Oharu had no idea what had happened. Once she had caught her breath, she said that when she had stopped in the corridor and had turned the light toward her master's feet, her right arm had suddenly gone numb and she dropped the lamp. In the darkness, someone had pounced on her from behind. Or rather, it was as if a demon had nestled up to her soundlessly and bound her entire body tightly with a spell, or as if a gigantic bear had crushed her against its chest. Though her head and mouth were being held tightly, she had managed to call out to her lord, but then she had received a sharp blow in the ribs and had passed out. Thus, if Lady Kikyō had not awakened and missed her husband and her attendant, the two might still have been lying in the corridor. By the time the lady and her attendants raised an outcry, the attacker had vanished without a trace, leaving only the vivid marks of the operation on Norishige's face. Mysteriously, he had stanched the wound and even applied a plaster to the flat center of the face before making his escape. Whether he wanted to act the surgeon in every respect or had some other reason for taking these steps, they were most kind and beneficial. For without them, the poor patient might have bled to death.

As you have probably guessed, this queer incident was the work of none other than Terukatsu. Of course, it was thanks to Lady Kikyō's guidance that his attack was so resoundingly successful. He and the lady had exchanged letters regularly by means of the underground passage, using Kaede and her daughter Oharu as messengers. No doubt one of the messengers would crawl through the tunnel and leave a letter wedged between the stones of the great wall; Terukatsu would pick it up on his rounds and leave a reply in the same place. Communication being maintained in this fashion, the time and place of the attack were arranged in advance so that Terukatsu could do his work quickly and return safely to the base of the stone wall without arousing suspicion.

In addition to the plaster he applied to Norishige's wound, he took a letter with him, which he placed on Norishige's face.

> For compelling reasons, I have sought your nose since last year. Tonight I have successfully realized my desire and am completely satisfied. I shall not take your life, and you may now set your mind at rest.

It is not clear how this message was interpreted by the senior retainers, but it was the product of Terukatsu's foresight. Once he had fulfilled the lady's commission, he hoped that security at the inner palace would be relaxed promptly and he would be able to approach the lady without difficulty; and so he sought with the letter to dispel everyone's anxiety.

Despite his thoughtful advice, however, the samurai were ordered to redouble their vigilance and the number of watch fires burning every night among the trees in the garden was increased. Since the incident had occurred during a month for which Terukatsu was head of the guard, he was of course called to account, but the senior retainers were in a quandary over his punishment. He had been assigned, after all, to guard the outer enclosure of the palace, and no one could be sure whether the assailant had entered the palace from outside or had been hiding inside. If there had been negligence, then it was negligence on everyone's part, and there were no grounds for singling out Terukatsu. Official suicide would have been inescapable if the lord had been killed, but only a bit of flesh had been lost. No lord, however great, would want to exchange a loyal retainer for a mere nose. In addition, the fact that Norishige's nose had been cut off was kept secret as much as possible— only a few palace maids and the senior retainers knew—so they could not blame anyone openly. And they had to exercise the greatest discretion, since they were dealing with Terukatsu, respected by everyone as a distinguished young warrior and the heir of Terukuni, Lord of Musashi. After considering all these factors they placed him in confinement for a time, and that was all; but he must have been in anguish, closed up in a room by himself, his thoughts racing to the scene in the inner palace. His ultimate goal was not the lady's revenge, but the tableau that would result from that revenge. His secret desire was to see the nose-less husband beside his incomparably beautiful wife. The world he had seen so long in his dreams would now be un-folding in the lady's bedchamber. This expectation sharply intensified his longing.

After a short time, he was released and permitted to re-turn to duty, but his anguish continued. If he were assigned again to the rotating monthly guard, he would be able to revisit the love tunnel at the base of the great wall, but he was no longer entrusted with that welcome duty; and, to make matters worse, the senior retainers were supervising what appeared to be a watertight guard, so that an ex-change of letters was out of the question, and he received not a breath of news, not even a rumor, of the state of affairs in the inner palace. It weighed on his mind, too, that, though he was on duty every day, he never saw Norishige. When he inquired, he was told that the retainers had not seen their lord since the time of the incident. Sometimes, it was true, Norishige would address his retainers from be-hind a reed blind in the audience room; but his speech was even fainter and harder to grasp than before, and his voice different, which led some to suspect a double and, quite naturally, to infer the worst. Terukatsu began to feel un-easy about the outcome of his surgery. He had taken such care in treating the wound; he thought surely Norishige must be all right. But aside from five or six administrators and a few personal attendants who knew the truth, no one had any evidence that their lord was still alive. If he could just see that Norishige was safe, thought Terukatsu, and learn the extent of the damage to his face, he would be able to assuage his thirst a bit by imagining the lady's satisfac-tion and the wicked smile in her eyes. And so he came to yearn for Norishige's noseless face as much as for the lady's.

In the Tenth Month of 1555—the year in which Norishige had been visited by one calamity after another—the era name was changed from Temmon to Kōji. Then the New Year came, and all the samurai to offer their greetings. The lord, however, without uttering a word of greeting, simply passed a congratulatory message from behind his reed blind; and the gloom of the old year continued into the new. Putting their heads together, the senior retainers agreed that morale would decline as long as their lord stayed shut up in his palace, and, most worrisome of all, ugly rumors would spread. A good, lively party might clear the air, but the lord would have to be persuaded to show his "noble countenance" to the assembled samurai. After all, the retainers were used to his harelip and missing ear, surely they would not be disconcerted by the loss of his nose. There was no reason to be so self-conscious. To a warrior, spirit is more important than appearance. What if his features were a little changed? None of the retainers was wrong-minded enough to despise his master for that. And so they cautiously felt him out on the idea, but Norishige, already seized with melancholy, had grown increasingly indecisive and timid since the latest incident and showed no inclination to appear before anyone. When they pressed him, he would say crossly, "Leaf me alone! If you wanna haf a farhy, ho aheah an' haf a farhy! Hon' hell me wha' 'oo hoo!" and withdraw.

One sometimes hears of disembodied voices, but Norishige's was not only disembodied; altered this way, his speech might have been taken for the cries of some animal. It would not be easy to convince the retainers that he was still alive. But some way had to be found to divert their lord, and finally the senior retainers decided to assemble all the samurai with a knowledge of poetry for a poetry party. For some time Norishige had been holding such gatherings in private with the ladies-in-waiting, but this one would be celebrated in grand style in the study of the outer palace. The idea originated with Lady Kikyō, and Norishige consented without a second thought, partly because the proposal came just as he was getting all puffed up over his own poetry, and particularly because it had been suggested by the lady. The senior retainers could come up with nothing else and, feeling quite out of their element at a poetry contest, feared that their choice would prove to be a great nuisance; but they would be happy if their lord's spirits brightened, and so conveyed his wishes to the samurai and announced that anyone with a knowledge of the art, without regard to station, would be allowed to attend. "Confessions of Dōami" records that:

> They chose the fifth of the Fifth Month, the day of the Iris Festival, to assemble the samurai in company with Lord Norishige and Lady Kikyō for a poetry party. They announced it far in advance and expected that everyone with a taste for the Way of Poetry would compose fine poems and vie for the prizes. But the warriors of Ojika Castle, though confident of their skill with a bow, were unaccustomed to elegant gatherings like this and hesitated to participate. They would compete in military events, they said, but had no desire to win honor with poetry. Few attended; no one liked the idea, and it was a cheerless affair.

Even in that turbulent age, a number of military leaders were proficient in poetry, it is true, but they were the well-educated sons of daimyo. Ordinary samurai were barely literate, and few of them would have enjoyed an elegant pastime like poetry. Terukatsu, in any case, was one of the handful of people at Ojika Castle qualified to attend the gathering. His surviving poems, when viewed as the work of a military man, maintain the proper conventions and show that he was well grounded in the art, but they are the fruit of diligent practice in his later years, after he had been inspired by this party to the realization that poetry was not to be slighted. At the time, he was a youth of nineteen and probably not particularly skilled at writing poetry. Nevertheless, he had been educated since childhood in both literary and military arts, while those around him were unschooled and illiterate. It is clear that he, more than anyone else, had an obligation to attend. When he heard that the gathering was the lady's idea, he must have hoped that she would provide him with an opportunity to renew their long-interrupted correspondence. Suppressing his excitement, he accepted the invitation.

Predictably, Norishige and his wife were hidden behind a reed blind on the dais while the retainers sat in rows on either side of the room. They competed in writing poems on the cuckoo, a topic chosen by the lady. Most of the retainers had been drawn by curiosity—perhaps they would see their master in person—but Norishige simply passed his own composition from behind the reed blind and listened quietly as it and then the retainers' poems were read aloud. If Terukatsu had been a noble in the Heian court, he might have used "cuckoo" (for it was an ideal topic) to convey his feelings indirectly to the beloved lady behind the reed blind. But he lacked the skill for that, and perfunctorily strung together thirty-one hackneyed syllables. Unfortunately, the poems written on this occasion have not survived, but it is safe to assume that none of them was of any merit. In "Confessions of Dōami" one poem by Lady Kikyō is preserved:

> *Reminded of the past*
> *By the scent of orange blossoms*
> *Come, O cuckoo*
> *To the village of falling blossoms.*

With a slight change in the last two lines, her poem is based on one by Prince Genji in the "Village of Falling Blossoms" chapter of *The Tale of Genji*:

> *Reminded of the past*
> *By the scent of orange blossoms*
> *The cuckoo comes to sing*
> *At the village of falling blossoms.*

Genji composed his poem when he visited Lady Reikeiden:

First he went to the lady's rooms, where they reminisced together as the night deepened; and when the third-quarter moon rose in the sky, the tall trees threw their shadows ever darker and the nostalgic scent of nearby orange blossoms wafted in. The lady had aged, but she was as modest as before, refined, and sweet. Though she had not been a special favorite of the late emperor, he had been fond of her and found her company relaxing.

Reikeiden replied to Genji's poems with one of her own:

> *No one ever calls*
> *At my weathered dwelling—*
> *The orange blossoms near the eaves*
> *Have drawn you here.*

But Lady Kikyō's poem bears no relation to these ancient matters. She simply likens the cuckoo to Terukatsu and makes a pun on *hana*, which means both "blossom" and "nose," so that "the village of falling blossoms" is also "the village of falling noses." Thus Terukatsu would have been able to grasp the underlying message, even though he probably had not read *The Tale of Genji*.

It is not clear just when Lady Kikyō was so moved by Terukatsu's devotion and strength of character that she began to reciprocate his love. But surely her poem conveys more than a simple "I want to see you, there is something we must discuss." Perhaps she came to love him, almost without realizing it, during the time they were unable to communicate. This poem may have been the first expression of her love.

> Because of the strict surveillance, I thought there would be little hope of even stealing close to her, but in time the guard was relaxed and I could visit her easily. A year had passed with no further trouble, as I had predicted in the letter I left behind that autumn night, and so the senior retainers finally put their doubts to rest.

They may have put their doubts to rest, but they never could figure out what the assailant had wanted with their master's nose.

Book V

❧❧ ❧❧ ❧❧ ❧❧ ❧❧

*In Which Terukatsu Returns to His Father's Castle
and Weds the Daughter of the Chirifu Clan*

Terukuni, Terukatsu's father, was old and in failing health,
and had been anxious for some time to find a suitable wife
for his son and retire as head of the clan. Again and again
he asked the Tsukuma to send his son back to the castle
on Mount Tamon. But there were alarming rumors; the
senior retainers at Ojika Castle had grown increasingly
suspicious, particularly since the rebellion at Tsukigata
Castle, and were slow to grant the request. Still, though
technically a hostage, Terukatsu had come to the castle
as a child and had lived there for fourteen or fifteen years.
He had served faithfully and repeatedly distinguished himself in battle, and there seemed to be no question of his
father's allegiance to the Tsukuma. Accordingly, Terukatsu
was finally permitted to return to Terukuni's palace in
the autumn of 1557.

Though he was happy, of course, to be going home to
his father, Terukatsu was a long time recovering from the
sorrow of his separation from Lady Kikyō. His warrior's
spirit reasserted itself in the face of necessity, but first love
is something special, even to a man of iron will. He had
violated all norms of morality and gratitude in his passionate devotion to her, and yet they were being forced apart
almost as soon as they had begun to meet. It had been the
autumn of the previous year that vigilance had finally become relaxed enough for him to use the tunnel again, and

so they had had less than one year together. Even then they had met in secret, living for brief moments of joy, probably without a single chance to pass the night in intimate conversation. Indeed, his regret was all the more intense in that his love was less for Lady Kikyō than for the unique role she enacted. In the future he might find other ladies as beautiful as she, but the strange and wonderful stage on which she was placed, particularly the drama that featured a comic supporting actor without a nose, was a world made to his order. He could hardly expect to find another noble lady with this setting and cast. And so Terukatsu, in his perverse lust, was reluctant to part with the lady and loath to withdraw from this environment. Their only consolation was a belief that the demise of the House of Tsukuma was not far off. They laid their plans for the future, pledged to meet again, and parted.

Lady Oetsu of the House of Chirifu, later known as Shōsetsuin, married into the House of Kiryū in the Third Month of 1558, less than six months after Terukatsu had returned to the castle on Mount Tamon. Terukatsu was twenty-one years old, and Shōsetsuin, fourteen. Though she was destined to pass her days in grief and loneliness, praying to the gods and buddhas that her husband's shameful sex life might be reformed, Oetsu was a vivacious young girl at the time of her wedding. If her body had felt the first stirrings of sexuality, she was not yet conscious of it, and her husband made no effort to enlighten her. His mind was filled with thoughts of the inner palace at Mount Ojika, and he could see his bride, whom he had taken only at his father's urging, as nothing more than an intelligent, innocent girl seven years his junior. But perhaps, after all, he was fortunate to have a bride too young to understand.

One summer evening a month or two after the wedding,

Terukatsu unexpectedly joined Shōsetsuin on the verandah as she was enjoying the cool air with her ladies-in-waiting.

"Let's do something amusing together, shall we?" he said, with an uncharacteristic grin.

"But how is your father?" she asked.

"There's nothing to worry about. He's been much better the last few days. What concerns me is the way I've been neglecting you. I'm free today, and I'll keep you company in whatever you want to do."

Shōsetsuin gazed happily at her cheerful husband.

"What shall we do, then?"

"Anything at all. What would you like?"

"Shall we hunt fireflies? Out in the garden?"

Her lovely, bright eyes filled with the sudden joy that comes to a child who has just thought of something wonderful. Her plump cheeks glowed.

"There are lots of fireflies in the garden, over where the flags are blooming, beyond the hill." She spoke just like a child.

Taking the ladies-in-waiting with them, the young couple eagerly chased fireflies about the garden.

"Over here, over here! Everybody come here!" Shōsetsuin's bright voice rang out amid the shrieks of her attendants as she rushed about, now to a clump of grass, now to the water's edge. As the daughter of a feudal lord, she had been reared to be a proper young lady, but at fourteen her arms and legs were stretching and her body was in the prime of health and vigor. Though her voluminous robes were a bit of a nuisance, she ran like a young deer around the garden. To the attendants watching her, it seemed too comical to address her as "Madam," she was so much the little girl.

"I've already caught ten," Terukatsu cried out wildly.

"Oh! I only have five!"

"There's one, there's one—I'm going to get him!" She was right behind Terukatsu as he darted off in pursuit. Running around the pond and along the stream, competing for the same firefly, they looked more like a brother and sister at play than newlyweds.

That night the young couple put their fireflies, some thirty or forty of them, in wicker cages set in a row to look at as they celebrated with sake. Both of them were still in a playful mood. Terukatsu began to tell jokes and silly stories that made Shōsetsuin laugh so she could hardly eat. The attendants were more amused by their master's rare show of spontaneity than by the stories themselves. They responded with peals of laughter every time he opened his mouth.

"Wait, wait," said Terukatsu. "Now I'm going to show you something funny." He nodded and whispered to one of the ladies-in-waiting.

Shōsetsuin and the others turned their eyes toward a cringing man that the attendant escorted to a matted corridor outside the room, and gazed at his shaven head as it scraped the mats in an abject bow. The freshly shaven pate gleamed.

"Ah, there you are," said Terukatsu.

"Yes, sir," the shaven head replied in a doleful voice.

"Who is that?" asked Shōsetsuin.

"His name is Dōami. We'll have him do something funny for us tonight." Turning to Dōami, he said sharply, "There, raise your head."

"Yes, sir." He replied in the same voice as before.

"Numbskull, don't just say 'Yes, sir.' I told you to raise your head!"

"Yes, sir." This time Dōami's head bobbed up as he spoke. About thirty years old, he dressed like a Buddhist priest, as was customary for a "tea steward." He was chubby and had a round, white face. He stared at them with his big eyes wide open as if he were startled. There was something droll about the oddly serious expression he had assumed and, when somebody tittered at the sight of him, all the attendants broke into giggles.

"Here, here, don't laugh yet." After restraining the women, Terukatsu spoke to Dōami.

"Well now, here's a chance to show us what you can do. Give it a try."

"It, sir? What do you mean by 'it'?" Like a dog watching for a signal from his master, Dōami looked up at Terukatsu and blinked his eyes rapidly.

"Ha, ha, ha, nincompoop. You're good at imitations, aren't you? Birds, insects, animals, people. You can imitate their voices, movements, everything. You're a clever fellow, go ahead."

"May I speak to him?" said Shōsetsuin.

"Ask him anything at all. Yes, that's good, you give him his instructions."

"Dōami, can you imitate anything at all?"

"I am overwhelmed, Your Ladyship. Oh, what shall I do?" With tears and distress in his voice, he pressed his shaven head to the mat again. "Oh dear, oh dear," he moaned. "What an extraordinary thing you have been told. Forgive me, Your Ladyship, but I have no such skill."

"Come, come, don't lie to her. You've performed for me often enough."

"What a cruel thing to say, My Lord. How could I do those things before Her Ladyship and these other ladies? You are too heartless."

"Ha, ha, ha, ha. 'The able falcon hides his talons,' doesn't he."

"P-p-please, My Lord, you are joking."

"Go ahead, get on with it. That's why I called you here."
"Dōami, imitate a firefly for me." Shōsetsuin's eyes flashed
mischievously.

Dōami is, of course, the author of that precious narrative
of the Lord of Musashi's career, "Confessions of Dōami."
For some time he had served in the offices of the castle,
capitalizing on his wit and charm; but this was the first
time he had been summoned to entertain at the young lady's
palace. He gives this account:

> I went in my youth to serve at the castle on Mount Tamon.
> At first I worked in the samurai quarters. Lord Terukatsu
> noticed me and said I was an amusing fellow. In my grati-
> tude I did my best to please him, and one day he sum-
> moned me to say that he wished me to perform that night
> for the diversion of the ladies, because I was good at doing
> imitations. I was taken to the inner palace and had the
> honor of coming before Lady Shōsetsuin herself.

Shōsetsuin's request was an exceedingly difficult one.
"What did you say?" Dōami sobbed. "Imitate a firefly? . . .
A firefly?" He rambled on in a tearful voice until everyone
was quite exasperated with him. This was his usual routine.
As he temporized, he would think of a trick to impress his
audience. He waited until the attendants noisily urged him
on, then, affecting a look of despair, he stood up and
fetched a fan from someplace. Going to a dark side of the
room, he began to chase his own shaven head with the fan.
When the fan came down with a slap, the head would glide
out from under it and escape. His blinking eyes and wonderful expressions perfectly conveyed the image of a firefly
glowing and fading, glowing and fading. The hand holding
the fan, hot in pursuit of the firefly, seemed to belong
to someone else. Finally the hand succeeded in pinning
down the head with the fan, and the head tried frantically

to escape. With the fan flapping after it, the head would break away, only to be caught again. The illusion of someone chasing a firefly was so perfect that it was hard to believe that this was simply one man's stunt. Terukatsu's plan worked. Marveling at the strange man who had appeared before them, Shōsetsuin and the ladies-in-waiting were convulsed with laughter from the beginning of his performance to the end. The firefly was followed by a number of other disconcerting requests, to each of which he responded with a whimper and a show of distress. It turned out that nothing was too difficult for him. He would capture some momentary quirk of the most difficult bird, animal, or insect, and convey it to the delighted audience with his voice and gestures. He was a master of facial expressions. With the slightest eye movement, wrinkle, or twist of the mouth, he could suggest a mood, a shape, a movement, even a color. Like a seasoned performer, he had learned to read his audience for signs of flagging interest and, when these appeared, to counter them with a change of pace. Just as the ladies began to think they had seen enough, he left off animal imitations and started to do drunks, halfwits, blind men, and the like, giving rise to new peals of laughter.

Shōsetsuin, who was at that age when everything is hilarious, had never seen anyone so clever and comical as this before. With tears in her eyes, she held her sides and gasped, "Oh, it hurts, it hurts." She immediately took a fancy to Dōami. "I have never laughed so much as I did tonight," she said to Terukatsu when the entertainment was over. "What a funny man. I would never be bored with him around."

"Ha, ha, ha. Was he really that good?"

"Yes, yes. Won't you call him here sometimes?"

"All right, if you like him you can take him into your service. He's better suited to the inner palace anyway." Terukatsu laughed happily.

At Shōsetsuin's request, Dōami was transferred to the private staff, where he occupied the same position as a blind masseur or a musician would: his job was to divert and entertain the ladies, and before long his wit and good humor had made him popular with everyone. There was constant merriment in the inner palace.

Terukatsu spent more and more time in his wife's room. "I miss Dōami," he would say, and, carried away by Dōami's antics, he would sometimes join in the most inane horseplay. To Shōsetsuin he had always been a rather distant husband, but now she sensed that he was casting off his former reserve. She attributed the change to the lighthearted Dōami, and grew even more partial to him.

As Terukatsu was drinking with his wife one evening, he said, "You shouldn't spend all your time listening to Dōami's banter. Tonight I'll tell you something educational."

"Something educational?"

"That's right. You have an easy life here, but what would you do, for example, if this castle were besieged by an enemy? Women have to help too when there's fighting. Shall I tell you what you ought to know?"

"Oh, yes. That is a good idea. Do tell us, please." Shōsetsuin unconsciously sat up straight; she thought she recognized the commanding look of a brave warrior in her husband's unusually serious countenance.

"Women don't have to go out on the battlefield. But during a siege, they have their own jobs to perform." Terukatsu began his lecture with the siege of Ojika Castle that he had witnessed, as a boy of twelve, in the fall of 1549.

"For instance, there is what's called 'dressing the heads.'"

Gradually bringing his account to the scene in the attic, he gave a detailed explanation of how the heads were washed, how the hair was dressed, how the labels were affixed, and so on. His wife and the four or five ladies in attendance listened eagerly, peering at Terukatsu's face as he spoke; and little by little, stimulated by his audience, he seemed to warm to the subject. It was rare for him to settle down and take the time to talk like this. As he spoke, there was a mysterious, grave power in his eloquence, and each word was delivered with authority. For good measure—when had he learned the art?—he painted a masterly verbal picture of the heads he had seen in the attic, their expressions, the color of their skin, the smears of blood, even the smell, until they seemed palpable before the ladies' eyes. Shōsetsuin and her attendants were first of all astonished by his memory and unexpected skill at storytelling, and then were drawn into the feeling that they were present in the attic. They listened breathlessly, unconsciously clenching their sweaty fists and stiffening their bodies. Just as they seemed to be swallowed up in Terukatsu's oddly glittering pupils, he said, "No, you won't understand if I just tell you about it." He began to look around the hushed, eerie room, searching out the dark corners into which the lamplight did not penetrate. The ladies were struck with terror. The words had come from Terukatsu's mouth, but the tone and pitch were suddenly different. Something new and peculiar had come into this voice. And then a twitching, trembling, incomprehensible smile rose straining to his lips. He suddenly went pale. Then he flushed brightly as if the blood had rushed to his head.

"That's right, you would understand headdressing if you had some practice. But for that we need a real head."

"A real head?" Shōsetsuin's voice betrayed her alarm.

"Are you afraid to look at a head?"

"No. But where would you get such a thing?"

"Ha, ha, ha. Aren't you the wife of a samurai? There's no hope for you if you turn pale at the mention of a head."

In fact, she was more frightened by her husband's feverish, possessed eyes than by looking at heads. She sensed an ominous incompatibility between his grin and those eyes. But when he challenged her, she drew herself up straight.

"No, no. I am not a coward. Heads do not frighten me."

"Are you sure?"

"Of course."

"Then you have the courage to look?"

"If you have one, please show it to me."

"Ah, I do have."

Then he turned to the ladies-in-waiting.

"Show your courage. I'm going to get a head and teach you what to do. I want you to practice. If you don't learn now, you'll be useless when the time comes."

His face suddenly went pale again. The ladies were thrown into confusion.

"Call Dōami," he cried, and emptied his sake cup at one gulp.

One night when I came before my master and Her Ladyship, Lord Terukatsu had me approach him closely. He said, "It's too bad for you, but tonight I want your head." He looked as though he were about to cut me down with his sword. I was astounded, having done nothing wrong, and I wailed and moaned, but he would not listen to me. There was no escape, I thought, and resigned myself; but Lady Shōsetsuin, who had always treated me with kindness, took pity on me and pleaded on my behalf. Suddenly he burst into roars of laughter. "I was only having fun. Why would I kill an innocent man?" he said. "You're a lucky fellow. But in exchange for sparing your life, I want you to play the part of a dead man and imitate a head, right here. Then it won't be necessary to kill you." What will become of me now, I thought in astonishment. He removed one mat from the floor of the room and had a two-foot opening cut in the boards under it. "Get in there and stick your head up through the hole," he said.

By allowing only his face to show above the hole, Dōami was to give the appearance of a head resting on the floor. This in itself may not have been particularly difficult for him, skilled mimic that he was. But imagine doing it for a very long time without moving so much as an eyelash. This was the role forced upon Dōami.

"Do you understand? You're to act exactly as though you were dead. You must stay perfectly motionless until I tell you otherwise. If you make the slightest movement I'll use my sword." Then, after pronouncing sentence on Dōami, Terukatsu turned to the ladies. "You are to treat it like the head of a dead man. You mustn't think of Dōami as being alive." Choosing three women, he assigned their respective tasks—washing the head, applying the makeup, and attaching the label.

When a pitcher, basin, head-board, table, incense burner, and the other props necessary to re-create the attic scene had been assembled, poor Dōami hid under the floor from the shoulders down and transformed himself into a silent, motionless head. His death's-head expression was very well done, but the better it was the more it reminded everyone of the trouble Dōami had in affecting it, and the result was rather comical. When the ladies considered that this glib entertainer was clenching his teeth in fear for his life, they felt less pity for him than a desire to try to make him sneeze. But to Dōami, the distress was nothing to laugh about. "Putting on a chagrined look, I fixed my eyes on a single point and kept my eyelids slightly open. I could not swallow the saliva that accumulated in my mouth, nor twist my face when my nostrils itched; but cruelest of all was that I could not blink. It would be better really to die, I thought, than to endure such agony." This complaint is uncharacteristic of him, and we must assume that the experience affected him deeply. The ordeal was all the more trying because the women twisted his head roughly this way and that as they practiced. But the easygoing Dōami could also be disdainful and, even as he was suffering, he took care to observe what went on in the room. His eyes, of course, were fixed on a single point, and things that barely entered his field of vision remained dimly at the corner of his eye. But, so far as possible, he paid close attention to the behavior of the people in the room, and watched and listened to everything that transpired.

What struck Dōami as most peculiar was the deadly seriousness with which Terukatsu viewed this idiotic quick course in headdressing. When the ridge of the comb went tap, tap on Dōami's head, the women were amused by his solemn imitation of a dead face and began to laugh in spite of themselves.

"Who was that," Terukatsu snapped. "Who laughed!" Anger flashed in his eyes. To maintain a sober atmosphere, he spoke in low tones and forbade the women to raise their voices. When someone failed to do exactly as he said, he would fly into a rage. Tonight's game was a little bizarre, the women thought. At first they suspected that the lord and Dōami had planned it as a prank to frighten them. Indeed, Dōami's head was not at all suitable as a practice piece, despite his skillful expression and the convincing way his head seemed to rest on the floor, because it was still attached to his torso and the women could not turn it over or carry it around. And his shaven pate ruled out any practice at dressing the hair. A melon would have been easier to use; at least they would have been spared the trouble of cutting a hole in the floor. But there seemed to be something behind Terukatsu's humorless intensity that night, and the women were uncertain whether or not he was joking. The same was true of Dōami in his role as the head. Maybe his master and the ladies were amusing themselves at his expense, he thought, but when he caught a glimpse of Terukatsu's face, there was no suggestion of playfulness in it. And the expression Dōami imagined there was particularly terrifying, as he could not see the face clearly; he only sensed its existence vaguely somewhere in his eye. Dōami's imagination was also stimulated by Terukatsu's voice. During the whispered lecture to the ladies, his voice was parched and shrill, like that of a feverish patient. It sounded tense, even effeminate. Dōami had never heard Terukatsu speak this way before. Ordinarily, he had a warrior's voice, deep and grand, forged on the battlefield; but tonight he spoke in an unnatural quaver, as though he were struggling to contain his agitation.

In any event, Dōami soon had good reason to be anxious. As he continued his lecture on headdressing, Terukatsu presently came to the subject of "woman-heads." "This head has a nose, it's not realistic enough," he said, pointing at Dōami. "I can't train you properly without a real woman-head." These words filled Dōami with dread. The lecture was moving in an ominous direction, and in the end his precious face might well be mutilated. He had escaped death, but it seemed that his nose could not be saved. Then, as if to confirm Dōami's fears, Terukatsu pinched the end of his nose.

"Here, here, bring me that razor," he said. "I might as well cut this thing off now. Then we'll have it nice and flat here, a real woman-head. I want everything to be authentic tonight."

This is it, thought Dōami, screwing up his resolve; but

Shōsetsuin and the ladies-in-waiting were too stunned to move. His wild, bloodshot eyes flashing, Terukatsu glared at the ladies as if he were inspecting them one by one.

"What are you doing? I told you to bring the razor!" His eyes rested on the most beautiful of the attendants, a girl of sixteen or seventeen named Ohisa. She shrank from his sharp gaze and bowed her plump, innocent face as if she were praying for the terror to pass quickly. But as Terukatsu stared at the glossy black hair that covered her shoulders and at the delicate, white fingers on her lap, a twitching smile crept to his lips again.

"Ohisa," he called. "Ohisa, bring the razor."

"Yes, sir." Her reply was almost inaudible. Still hanging her head, she rose; and as the silent air trembled in a gentle breeze, the lamplight cast flickering shadows on Dōami's face.

"Sit down here," Terukatsu said, motioning her in front of the head. "You cut. Hold the razor this way. That's right. Then cut the nose here. Keep it flat and neat."

"Yes, sir."

"Go ahead. This is the head of a dead man. There's nothing to be afraid of."

"Please forgive me, My Lord."

"That's enough! Cut! Cut, I say!"

Ohisa's hand trembled as she clutched the razor. She was terrified by Terukatsu's command, but Dōami's face frightened her more. Even now his eyes were riveted to a single spot, and his expression remained exactly as before. He was eerily still. Maybe he really was dead, she thought. She tried pressing and stroking the ridge of his nose. Her slender fingers came away cold and damp. Looking closely, she saw a cold sweat trickling from Dōami's forehead and down his temples. Then, when the blade of the razor gleamed before it, the death face suddenly went pale.

"My Lord." Now it was Shōsetsuin who spoke. "I beg you, please spare him."

"No. There's nothing to cutting off a dead man's nose. Ohisa will never be of any use to me if she's frightened by the sight of blood. I want to educate her."

"But think of poor Dōami. Just look at him. Aren't you impressed by the way he is obeying your orders? Please, please, consider his devotion and spare him."

"Ha, ha, ha." Terukatsu suddenly looked self-conscious and gave a weak laugh. "All right, all right. If you say so, I'll drop the idea."

"Oh, will you really?"

"Yes, but I have another idea."

What would he say next, they all wondered fearfully.

"Ha, ha, ha." Terukatsu's laugh was more cheerful now. "Don't worry. I was only joking when I said we'd cut off his nose. His imitation was so good that I wanted to give him a scare." Then he turned to Dōami. "Well done. You're following my orders exactly. In consideration of your good attitude, I'll let you keep your nose, but I'm going to paint it red. Ha, ha, ha, ha. How's that? Are you grateful? If you're grateful, say so."

The head remained as silent as a rock.

"Answer me! You have my permission to speak!"

"Yes, sir," Dōami said finally, but he maintained his deathly expression and threw his voice so that it seemed to come from somewhere else.

"Are you uncomfortable?"

"Yes, sir."

"But being uncomfortable is better than being cut, isn't it."

"Yes, sir."

"Ah, ha, ha, ha. He's funny."

Soon Ohisa had replaced the razor with rouge and a

brush. After she had painted Dōami's nose bright red, the young women forgot their fright of a moment before and began to giggle. As usual, Shōsetsuin's bright voice rang out. Gradually they were persuaded that Terukatsu had simply played a nasty trick and, in the end, Dōami became their plaything.

"Dōami, Dōami," they cried, striking him on the head. "Here! You're supposed to be dead." They pinched his ears and cheeks. "If you move, we'll tell His Lordship and have you killed."

It was only after they had done all their mischief and left the room that Dōami was finally allowed to crawl out of the hole in the floor and come back to life.

In Which Dōami Sheds Tears of Gratitude, and Shōsetsuin Grieves

Terukatsu's vagaries did not come to an end with that night. The next night, too, he was in a mischievous mood and, acting the little tyrant, incited Shōsetsuin and the ladies-in-waiting to join him in playing with Dōami's head. He had rouge applied to the nose and said, "Tonight let's look at it from bed." Abruptly he had bedding brought into the room and lay down with his wife to enjoy the view of Dōami's red nose.

For Dōami, this was even more of a trial than the night before. Then he had had to persevere through the evening hours but was free again late at night; this time he had to stand under the floor all night with his head protruding from the hole. His memoir gives the impression that the room was quite large, with the hole through which he showed his head roughly in the center. Terukatsu had Shōsetsuin's bedding spread ten or twelve feet from the hole, from

Dōami's head, and his own bedding a few feet beyond hers. It was summer, and so a delicate mosquito net was suspended over the beds of the young daimyo and his wife. A lamp was placed on either side of Dōami's head, and a folding screen behind it, so that the head could be seen clearly from within the mosquito net. Though he could dimly make out the soft surface of the net in the darkness, Dōami could see nothing of the couple inside.

But there was more to Dōami's suffering than that. After dismissing the attendants and retiring to bed, the couple started to drink again.

"Is that what a real woman-head looks like, My Lord?" asked Shōsetsuin. She was not a heavy drinker, but when she did become intoxicated she found everything amusing. Tonight she was in particularly high spirits, perhaps because her husband had pressed so many cups of sake on her.

"No, not at all. On a real woman-head there's a dark cavity instead of a red nose. Much more gruesome."

Shōsetsuin went into peals of laughter.

"Now that we're alone, doesn't that head frighten you a little?"

"Not a bit."

"What if I weren't here with you?"

"I would be fine, even if you were not here. What's so frightening about a head with a red nose? It only makes me laugh."

"And who was it that turned pale when I called for a razor last night?"

"That's a fib, a fib. How could you say such a thing!"

"But it's true. You were even whiter than Ohisa."

"Well, I felt sorry for Dōami, and so I asked you to stop. I was not afraid."

"I wonder."

"How mean! Do you think I'm such a coward?"

"If that were a head from a real corpse, you'd have the courage to cut off the nose by yourself?"

"Of course. I am much stronger than Ohisa. I wish you'd think of something more frightening than that. Something more challenging."

Their joking led somehow to the subject of lay-priest heads.

"By the way," said Terukatsu, "where do you suppose you attach the label to a bald head?"

"Where would you put it?"

"You make a hole in his ear and tie the label there."

"A hole in his ear!" Again she collapsed into laughter. "But I guess there's no other way, is there?"

"How about it? If you have the courage, give it a try. A little thing like that won't matter to anybody."

"What should I make the hole with?"

"An awl would do, or the tip of a knife. Just a little jab. It won't hurt at all."

"Yes, well, it's a bit cruel, but I think I'll try it."

"Go ahead, go ahead."

Laughter.

"Don't try to get out of it by laughing!"

"I'm not trying to get out of it. The more I look at that expression the more I want to do it."

"He seems to be saying, 'Please do it, please do it.' "

More laughter. "Are you sure it's all right?"

"Yes, of course."

"Dōami, can you hear us?" Shōsetsuin peeked outside the net. "Could you hear our conversation? You have my permission to answer."

"Yes, ma'am," Dōami's head replied.

"It's just a little jab. You can take that."

"Yes, ma'am."

"He says it hardly hurts at all."

"Yes, ma'am."

"When I think of you with that expression, and a label hanging from your ear, I just can't resist."

"Yes, ma'am, that's only natural."

"Now be quiet again."

Too much sake had caused her to drop her usual reserve, and she was speaking like a tomboy.

"Please come watch, My Lord."

"We have to make a label. Bring some paper and a knife."

"Yes, yes, I have them right here." She was already outside the net, taking a knife and paper from her writing box and laughing in delight. This is how Dōami describes what happened:

> His Lordship said to use my right ear. Lady Shōsetsuin took the lobe of my right ear in her snowy hand, examined my head for a moment, and gave a low, nasal laugh. Lord Terukatsu was watching from the side. "Are you frightened?" he asked. "Why should I be frightened?" she replied with a bright smile. "Look at this death-face expression. It's so amusing. He must be frightened out of his wits, but this imitation is marvelous. He doesn't look as though he were aware of anything that's going on." Taking the knife in her right hand, she jabbed my earlobe. A trickle of blood stained her linen-white hand. Even then, I kept as still as death. "What a patient creature he is," she said with a laugh. But perhaps, after all, her spirits were dampened, for with no further ado she attached the label hastily and hurried back inside the mosquito net with her husband. They went on talking far into the night, with the greatest warmth and intimacy.

He continues:

> I was never called upon to play a head again, and His Lordship had the hole in the floor covered. When I appeared before Lady Shōsetsuin some time later, she stared uncom-

fortably at the wound on my ear and said, "I drank more that night than a woman ought to. I was carried away by the sake and treated you cruelly. Please forgive me." "But I am filled with gratitude," I replied. "There was nothing to prevent you from killing a no-account like me but, instead, you spared my life. This little scratch is nothing at all. In fact, I shall never forget, not in this life or the next, that you touched me with your own hands." I sobbed in gratitude. There is still a scar on my right ear, but when I think of it as a reminder of the noble lady at play, this ear of mine does not seem to belong to me at all.

Is it possible that a woman as gentle and virtuous as Shōsetsuin ever made such a mistake? It is hard to believe, and one does not want to believe it; for it would be the only blemish on her thirty-some years of life. For the wife of a daimyo, on a drunken whim, to cut a hole in a living man's ear is enough, unless we keep it in perspective, to ruin her reputation and cast a shadow on a beautiful character. But I would ask the reader to keep in mind that she was a girl of fourteen and that it was her husband's stratagem, carefully devised far in advance, that induced her, step by step, into committing her mistake.

Terukatsu probably began to make his plans when he first became acquainted with Dōami. He changed his cool attitude toward Shōsetsuin and drew closer to her. Then he brought in Dōami and saw to it that he won the hearts of Shōsetsuin and her ladies. But it seems likely that his sole intent was to produce the "practice headdressing" scene. From the start, his objective must have been to make Dōami imitate a woman-head, to incite Shōsetsuin to cut a hole in his ear, and then to gaze at the head while he and his wife exchanged intimacies inside the mosquito net. In short, he re-created the scene he had been picturing in his fantasies ever since leaving the castle on Mount Ojika. Substituting Dōami for Norishige, and Shōsetsuin for Lady Kikyō, he allayed the anguish he had felt since parting from his first love.

Nevertheless, the fact that Shōsetsuin took pleasure, even momentarily, in tormenting Dōami, that she indulged in this outrageous game, so out of keeping with her ordinary conduct, would seem to attest to a predisposition in all women, if properly directed, to enjoy cruelty—a proclivity, in other words, for brutality. In most women, particularly in the case of a high-minded woman like Shōsetsuin, such behavior does not continue long. The account of her "uncomfortable" apology in "Confessions of Dōami" bespeaks how much Shōsetsuin repented of her sad error. Though she probably did not see through to the truth of her husband's insidious motives, she must have sensed that there was something strange in his actions and intuitively felt a vague terror and anxiety. If so, the most important cause would have been her experience that evening, when "they went on talking far into the night, with the greatest warmth and intimacy." The nun Myōkaku says in "The Dream of a Night" that Shōsetsuin never slept with the Lord of Musashi, but this is only Myōkaku's guess. The testimony of Dōami, who was just outside the mosquito net that night, leaves no room for doubt. It is clear enough that Terukatsu moved the bedding to that room because he intended to use the view of Dōami's head as a stimulus. It is common, in any case, for a naïve bride suddenly to regard men as disgusting, and so we can imagine what impression Terukatsu made on Shōsetsuin with this mischief. It is true that she joined in the fun while she was drunk, but once she returned to her senses, the memory of those nightmarish hours must have terrified her. No doubt she sensed, if only vaguely, that there was something ominous in her husband's conduct. Terukatsu probably wanted to play the game the next night, too, but his desires were frustrated after that first evening. As Dōami says, "I was never called upon to play a head again, and His Lordship had the hole in the floor covered." In the interval, then, the feelings of the young couple had become estranged. However eager he may have been in his pursuit of pleasure, Terukatsu lacked the courage, when confronted with the saintly Shōsetsuin's grief and remorse, to debase her again.

Book VI

🏴 🏴 🏴 🏴 🏴

In Which Ojika Castle Falls, and
Norishige Is Taken Prisoner

The *Tsukuma War Chronicles* contain this account:

Lord Norishige, pleading ill health, had for several years
entrusted the governance of his domain to the senior retainers and retired to the inner palace, where his love for
Lady Kikyō caused him utterly to forget affairs of state.
The days and nights were not long enough for him to get
his fill of pleasure from the "green curtains and crimson
bedchamber," and everyone, from the samurai to the
townspeople, was uneasy about the fate of the House of
Tsukuma. Suddenly, in the First Month of 1559, Lord
Norishige ordered a campaign against the adherents of the
Higaki Temple in Asanuma District and dispatched Shida
Tōminokami with three thousand cavalry to subdue them.
The background of this action can be traced to the autumn
of 1557, when a senior retainer of the Yakushiji House,
named Baba Izuminokami, usurped his master's position
with help from the forces of the Ishiyama Hongan Temple.
Lord Masahide, thus deprived of his ancestral domain, fled
from the port of Sakai to the central provinces, and disappeared without a trace. Lady Kikyō, Lord Norishige's
wife and Lord Masahide's younger sister, was deeply distressed. Through the good offices of the Shogunate, the
Houses of Tsukuma and Yakushiji had been tied by
marriage and pledges of firm friendship exchanged for
years; yet Lord Norishige, despite the collapse of the
House of Yakushiji, overlooked Baba's treachery and did

nothing to avenge his wife's family. Such inaction was a disgrace to a warrior family, Lady Kikyō thought, but Lord Norishige, in his present condition, lacked the strength to do anything. She could only grieve over having such a useless husband. One night, in spite of herself, she let tears fall on her husband's face as he slept. Lord Norishige awakened and asked in surprise why she was crying. At first she was inconsolable and made no reply, but finally she raised her head. "The house of my father and my ancestors has been overthrown by a traitorous vassal and my only brother has disappeared. Now I grieve because I am about to lose even my husband to that same Baba." She began to sob uncontrollably. Greatly astonished, Lord Norishige pressed for more information. Lady Kikyō said that Baba had won the Higaki adherents to his side and was plotting with them to overthrow the Tsukuma. As evidence, she showed him a secret message. He opened the document and read it. It appeared to be a letter from the Higaki Temple to Baba, a clear invitation to invade the Tsukuma domain from the east and west. When he asked how she had obtained the letter, she said that a former Yakushiji retainer, Matoba Shinzaburō (a son of the lady's nurse), had chanced upon the message and passed it on to his mother. Lord Norishige, thinking it a matter of grave concern, quickly assembled his senior retainers and expressed his alarm. The retainers pointed out that the Higaki adherents had, for many years, been particularly cordial and had served with unparalleled devotion for generations. It did not stand to reason, therefore, that they would side with the traitor Baba and draw their bows against the Tsukuma. The letter should not be believed uncritically, the retainers concluded, nor should a campaign be launched without careful deliberation. Lord Norishige listened. Then asking, "Do you doubt my wife?" he angrily retired to his chambers. Thereafter Lady Kikyō continued her laments, pleading night after night, "Even if you are unsure about this letter, the Higaki people are certainly your enemies. It is well known that their comrades in the Ikkō sect joined forces with Baba to drive my brother out. Please do not wait any longer to put them to death." Word of these concerns somehow reached Higaki at about the same time. The adherents were surprised. In all the years of alliance they had never harbored treacherous designs against the Tsukuma lords, and so it was most disturbing for them to think that a punitive force might, for no reason, be sent against them. It would be better, they decided, to launch their own attack and prove their courage than to wait idly and be destroyed. Toward the end of 1558, they began to raise a large force.

The fall of Ojika Castle probably did begin with the attack on the Ikkō sect, as the official history says. But we can assume that it was the Lord of Musashi, working behind the scenes, who induced Lady Kikyō to prevail with Norishige, and ultimately to bring about a confrontation with the Higaki adherents. For Terukuni, Lord of Musashi, had died in the Tenth Month of 1558 at the castle on Mount Tamon. Terukatsu succeeded his father as head of the clan and assumed the title of Lord of Musashi; and, as there was no longer anyone to check his ambition, he was able to make whatever plans he liked. It goes without saying that his first target was the imbecile lord on Mount Ojika, the noseless, earless Tsukuma Norishige waiting, with folded arms, to be destroyed. Burning with a lust for territory, the Lord of Musashi surveyed his neighbors with the eye of a hungry tiger and saw the ideal prey. If he let the opportunity pass, someone else would certainly make a move. There was no reason to hesitate. He would anticipate the others and take the Tsukuma domain for himself. Yet surely the Lord of Musashi was motivated by more than ambition. In his heart of hearts stirred something quite unrelated to his aspirations as a military leader—a sweet, gentle, unquenchable love. We must consider that his honeymoon life with Shōsetsuin ended in frustration before three months were up. Having failed in the attempt to form his bride in the mold he preferred, he apparently was drawn again, with even greater intensity, to his lover at Mount Ojika. And to satisfy his love, nothing could be better than to topple the stronghold of the Tsukuma clan and to seize all of Norishige's possessions, including his wife, for himself. Territorial lust and physical lust coincided once again, and the latter, though one should never draw hasty conclusions about a great man's motives, may well have been the greater spur to action.

Now as for the authenticity of the message that Lady Kikyō showed Norishige—the appeal from the Higaki adherents to Baba Izuminokami: it is nowhere stated unequivocally, but the circumstances make it clear that the letter was a forgery. We can assume, too, that the Matoba Shinzaburō mentioned in the *Chronicles* was a younger brother of Matoba Zusho and Matoba Daisuke, and that Lady Kikyō and the Lord of Musashi, acting in collusion, entrusted the forged letter to him and plotted the estrangement of Mount Ojika from the Higaki Temple. So it was, then, that in the First Month of 1559 Shida Tōminokami's army marched off toward Asanuma District on Norishige's orders. But the Higaki adherents incited the local peasants to rise up in revolt, and then engaged the attacking army on the bed of the Asade River at the boundary between the Tsukuma and Higaki domains. In a furious battle, the Tsukuma force, though twice as numerous as the enemy, was crushed. They fled back to Ojika Castle. The castle dispatched another army, only to be defeated again. Flushed with victory, the Higaki forces went on a rampage through the domain, and within a month had captured a number of subsidiary castles. The men of the Ikkō sect had been stirred to action by a threat to their existence, and had been on the defensive; but they learned in battle how weak the enemy really was and, little by little, their confidence swelled. In part, their success could be attributed to their formidable armaments and strength. But it was also evidence of the Tsukuma clan's loss of authority, of misgovernment throughout the domain, and of the collapse of the warriors' morale. In Ikkansai's day, Ikkō monks on a rampage would not have caused such a furor. The senior retainers at Mount Ojika viewed this state of affairs in consternation. If the monks were not subjugated at once, the domain would flare up like a nest of angry hornets. It was clear that Yokowa Buzen, who had raised an insurrection at Tsukigata Castle five years before, had already established contact with the rampaging monks and was about to move. Soon Baba, too, would become involved. Since nothing but the total subjugation of the rebels would do, the head of the senior retainers, Tsukuma Shōgen Haruhisa, was entrusted with a force of more than ten thousand. In the districts of Asanuma, Kuryū, and Shiihara, he routed the peasant rebels and closed in on their home base from three sides. The Higaki force, though even larger than before, was only one third the size of the Tsukuma army, and they were eventually forced to retreat to their stronghold in Asanuma. There they could only raise the walls, deepen the moat, and try to defend themselves. The standoff continued for six weeks, until in the Fifth Month the Higaki leaders officially requested help from the master of Mount Tamon, the Lord of Musashi.

Asanuma District, where the Higaki forces had entrenched themselves, lay between the Tsukuma and Musashi estates, with the Tsukuma to the west and the Lord of Musashi to the east. As Tsukuma Shōgen set out on his punitive expedition, he dispatched a messenger to Mount Tamon with an order to attack the rebels from the rear, but the Lord of Musashi gracefully declined. In his reply he said, "My clan has been indebted to Lord Tsukuma since the time of my father, Terukuni, and so in the present situation I want to do everything possible to help. Unfortunately, we have been devout converts to the Ikkō sect since the time of my great-grandfather, and we have a special relationship with the Higaki people. Our association with the House of Tsukuma, then, is of two generations' duration, and that with the Ikkō sect, four generations. Accordingly, if I had to ally myself with one side or the other, I would be obliged to choose the Higaki. But, as that is not my true desire, I beg to be allowed to remain neutral, thereby satisfying my obligations to both sides." Probably this was no more than a pretext. The Tsukuma leaders at Mount Ojika were worried about Baba Izuminokami because of the secret message, and suspected him of manipulating the Higaki uprising; but there is no evidence that Baba was involved, and so our suspicions fall on the Lord of Musashi. His neutrality is extremely suspect, and there is little doubt but that he was secretly backing the Higaki. When they came to him for help, he pretended to decline once or twice, in a roundabout way, pleading his painful dilemma; but later, as a steady stream of messengers brought their requests for help, he finally threw off his mask and revealed his determination to aid the Ikkō adherents. "Until now, out of gratitude to Ikkansai, I have declined the entreaties of the Higaki people. But I have lost all patience with the inaction and incompetence of the Tsukuma clan. They have attacked a force of several thousand with an army three times as large, yet in nearly six months they have not accomplished their goal. The lord and retainers on Mount Ojika are disgracing the memory of Ikkansai. It is perfectly clear to me that they will soon lose their domain and bring ruin upon the clan. I can no longer bear to stand aside and watch this spectacle. I have decided to aid the Higaki people and rescue the peasants from the misgovernment and turmoil under which they are suffering. I am indebted to Ikkansai, it is true, but why should I hesitate to replace imbeciles like these?" Summoning a Tsukuma messenger who had just arrived with a letter from Norishige, the lord made this haughty declaration. He added, "Go tell Norishige what I have said," and promptly sent the messenger back to Mount Ojika.

The Lord of Musashi was now twenty-two years old. He had been to war several times, but this was his first opportunity to ride at the head of a select army as commander in chief and lord of the domain. Several years of secret planning had produced the desired results. The times were ripe for a new hero to appear on the battlefield. Fame would be his; power and love were before his eyes, waiting for him to seize them. It is not difficult to imagine the satisfaction he must have felt. In the middle of the Sixth Month, he set out from Mount Tamon with eight thousand cavalry and joined the Higaki forces in Asanuma District; but the Tsukuma, unwilling to continue their fruitless offensive, struck camp without putting up a fight, enabling the Lord of Musashi and the Higaki forces to recapture Kuryū and Shiihara districts at once. As the allied forces advanced in pursuit of the enemy, many of the castle lords along the way saw how the wind was blowing and joined them. Tsukigata Castle, too, unfurled the standard of rebellion and set about subduing its neighbors. But the details of these campaigns are related in the *Tsukuma War Chronicles*, and we need not go into them here. In constant communication with each other, the allied forces from the east and Yokowa Buzen from the south closed in on the Tsukuma domain until they came together and surrounded Ojika Castle. This was in the Eighth Month of 1559, exactly ten years after Yakushiji Danjō Masataka had laid siege to the castle.

The combined forces of the Lord of Musashi, the Higaki, and Yokowa numbered about the same as the Yakushiji army, some twenty thousand. At first, seven or eight thousand defenders stood inside the castle, but as the number of refugees and surrendering troops grew, the force dwindled to a paltry three or four thousand. Under Ikkansai, the castle had held out for two months and finally had been able to avoid defeat; but this time the attack began on the fifteenth, the third citadel was taken on the twenty-first, the second citadel on the twenty-fifth, and the keep itself on the twenty-seventh. Only eleven days had elapsed. According to the *Tsukuma War Chronicles*, Norishige remained secluded in the inner palace throughout the siege, trusting the senior retainers to direct the fighting; but in the middle of the night of the twenty-second, he realized that the castle could not hold out much longer. Committing his eight-year-old son and six-year-old daughter to their nurse, he sent them off to a secret refuge. Late in the morning of the twenty-seventh, when told that the enemy had entered the keep, he calmly exchanged a cup of sake with his wife and composed a death verse. Then, according to the *Chronicles*, he set fire to the inner palace, stabbed his beloved wife to death, and took his own life. But if we believe "The Dream of a Night" and "Confessions of Dōami," this account cannot be true. It says that Norishige disemboweled himself, but it does not name the second who cut off his head. And, according to the *Chronicles*, no trace was ever found of the couple's remains, despite a thorough search of the charred ruins. This sort of thing is not unheard of. There is a story that Mitsuhide was greatly upset when Nobunaga's head could not be found at the time of the Honnōji Incident of 1582. But if the heads and bodies at Mount Ojika were reduced totally to ashes, who reported the death verses, so conspicuously included in the *Chronicles?* Norishige was loath to have anyone see his face and allowed no one near him but his wife. It is odd, too, that the verses of the ladies-in-waiting are preserved in the records, even though their authors are supposed to have perished in the conflagration. It is not inconceivable that someone forged the verses, thinking that, because Norishige had been so addicted to poetry, it was imperative to have a death verse. In any case, the author of the *Tsukuma War Chronicles* must have been a Tsukuma retainer, and we may assume that, even had he known the truth, he would not have written anything that would bring discredit on the clan.

Recognizing the official version for what it is, then, let us turn to the account in "Confessions of Dōami." When the Lord of Musashi broke down the gates and entered the keep on the morning of the twenty-seventh, he saw flames shoot up from the inner palace. Scattering the foot soldiers that descended upon him, he rushed to the love tunnel at the base of the great stone wall. Shedding his armor outside the opening, he made his way lightly through the tunnel and, choking in the swirling smoke, ran through the corridors to Norishige's chambers.

"Excuse me," he said, and kicked in the shoji. Norishige was about to stab his wife in the breast, but Terukatsu seized his arm violently.

"Let ho! Let ho, I hay!" Taken completely by surprise, Norishige had no time to look at the strange man who had appeared suddenly out of the smoke; he could only struggle frantically.

"Don't be rash, My Lord!" While he was shouting at the desperate Norishige, Terukatsu freed the lady's collar from her husband's grip. To shield her, he forced his way between them.

"It's Heruhatsu!" Norishige cried out in surprise. Thoroughly embarrassed, he blinked as though he had been slapped in the face. Terukatsu, seeing his chance, grabbed the sword from Norishige's hand. Then, making every effort not to look at Norishige's face, he moved back to a respectful distance and bowed deeply.

From Norishige's point of view, Terukatsu was an enemy to be hated. He had betrayed his debt to Ikkansai and forced Norishige into this predicament. But Norishige had not expected his enemy to pop up in a place like this. When their eyes met, he thought, "Ah, he's seen my face," feeling more embarrassment than hatred. The truth is that when Terukatsu had been visiting the lady's bedroom every night, she had often allowed him ecstatic peeks at the grotesque face, and he was not seeing it for the first time; but Norishige had no way of knowing this. He thought he had successfully concealed the loss of his nose, but now, to his resentment and chagrin, he had been seen by the enemy just as he was about to end his life, and all his caution had come to naught. He was utterly dejected. More than anything else, he was afraid of disgracing his family name. The inept son who had undone the great accomplishments of his forebears, he was prepared to expiate his failures by killing himself; but if he were to die now, his head would fall into Terukatsu's hands. Then it would be displayed before the public gaze, and people would ask, "How could he go on living with a face like that?" He could bear his own disgrace, but how could he avoid sullying the illustrious memory of his ancestors? He had no idea which way to turn. He could not go on living, nor could he die under these circumstances. His plan had been to kill his wife and plunge into the flames so that nothing would remain of his ugly form. But if his head were taken, he would not be able to face his father in the other world. Straightaway the hot-tempered old man would shout, "Idiot! Go get your nose and your ear!"

"He-He-Heruhatsu!"

"Yes, sir." He bowed even lower than before.

"I affeal hoo you hymhahy as a hamurai. Hiv hah my hword! An hone hay my heh!" In his excitement, Norishige was even more difficult to understand than usual. He seemed to be saying, "I appeal to your sympathy as a samurai. Give back my sword! And don't take my head!"

Having figured out this much, Terukatsu replied gently, "It is my sympathy as a samurai that compels me to stop you." He spoke with all the courtesy due his former master. "I am sorry to say this, but soon the attackers will force their way in here. If you kill yourself, someone will surely find your head, even if I do not take it. Think of the disgrace to generations past and future."

"He-He-Heruhatsu!"

"Yes, sir."

"My lash rehesh! He my hehon! Hu-hury my heh ho ho one will hee it!"

"What? What did you say?"

Seeing that Terukatsu did not know how to respond, Norishige repeated frantically, "My lash rehesh . . . my lash rehesh. . . ." Exasperated, he stretched his neck and made a cutting motion with his hand. "My heh! my heh!" Terukatsu finally realized that he was saying, "My last request! Be my second and bury my head so no one will see it!" But by now the fire was burning near them, and the wind, moaning through cracks all around, threw up terrible flames. Joined by some strange, ill-fated bond, Lady Kikyō, Norishige, and the Lord of Musashi might have been happier had they been swallowed up in that vortex of hellfire.

Norishige, at least, must have desired it, and Lady Kikyō may well have thought that she could uphold her duty to both men by dying with them in the flames. Her revenge was complete, her father's rancor assuaged. Taking her noseless, harelipped, one-eared husband along to the nether-world would be the best possible present for her father. Certainly that would be better than living on in this world, disgraced and piling up sin. But the Lord of Musashi, alone among them, had the will and ardor to resist the fire. He had left a company of soldiers with Aoki Shuzen, who knew the castle well, and instructed him to hurry directly to the inner palace. Fighting his way through the raging flames, Shuzen arrived at just the right moment. Simultane-ously, five or six pages, having followed their master through the secret underground passage, came bursting in.

"Leave everything to me, My Lord," said Terukatsu, standing up, and on this signal Shuzen's soldiers noiselessly surrounded Norishige. The hero of this comical, pathetic scene was seized by the arms and legs and carried out through the garden to the secret mountain path.

Lady Kikyō, of course, was rescued with the others. But only the handful of soldiers who had rushed to the inner palace knew the truth, while the Higaki and Yokowa forces, and most of the Lord of Musashi's men, believed that Norishige and his wife had perished in the fire. Ac-cording to "Confessions of Dōami," Norishige and the lady were secretly transferred to the castle on Mount Tamon and installed in a refurbished mansion deep in a place called Third Valley; to all the vassals it was known as the Third Valley Palace, but none of them knew who lived there, nor were any but Dōami and a few attendants aware that the Lord of Musashi often went there late at night. It might be thought exceedingly fainthearted of Norishige to have gone on living under these circumstances, ignominiously taken prisoner and passing the gloomy months and years in his enemy's castle, but the fact is that he was closely watched day and night, and all means of suicide had been removed. He had no opportunity to disembowel himself, nor would there have been any way for him to prevent others from seeing his face had he died; and so, unavoidably, he clung to his remaining years. But, domestically, the years in the Third Valley Palace may have been the happiest in Norishige's unfortunate life. There was no longer any need for him to bother his head over military and governmental affairs, for which he was unsuited in any case, and his compassionate enemy provided for all his needs. In particular, Norishige's daughter Oura, whom he had sent away with her brother just before the fall of Ojika Castle, was brought to the mansion (the boy, it seems, had been found and secretly killed), so that the three, father, mother, and daughter, could comfort one another in their loneliness and enjoy a quiet family life. Lady Kikyō, moreover, underwent a change of heart after the fall of the castle. Abandoning the cruelty by which she had taken pleasure in her husband's ruin, she returned to her true, feminine nature, and, feeling real pity and sympathy for her husband's ugliness, to which she had contributed, she strove as a faithful wife and loving mother to redeem her former indiscretions. And so for the first time a complete love developed between them, and Norishige lived with an emotional fulfillment such as he had never experienced before.

But Lady Kikyō's change of heart meant that the Lord of Musashi's fantasies ended in frustration. Spurred by ambition and love, he had defeated the House of Tsukuma and could enjoy his trysts without any concern for the opinions of others. His disappointment must have been intense when, after bringing his lover to his castle, he saw that her feelings were not as they had been. And it is quite natural that Lady Kikyō lacked the heart to resume their liaison. Having avenged her father, she no longer bore her husband any ill will, and she must have shuddered at the monstrous sins she had committed. Another view is that Lady Kikyō's sudden coolness to the Lord of Musashi arose from his having broken his promise and murdered Norishige's heir. Perhaps this is so, for one of her objectives in turning to him in the first place had been to elicit his support in bringing up the children, particularly the boy, as fine samurai, thereby maintaining the Tsukuma line.

And so the affair between the Lord of Musashi and Lady Kikyō broke off when she moved to the Third Valley Palace. To the end of his forty-two years, the lord sought out new women, one after another, with whom to share his bizarre stimulus and revolting dissipation. But that story would be too long and would detract from the lord's memory. The prudent thing would be to divulge no more. Once you know about the secret side of the Lord of Musashi's sexual life, you will, I am sure, make many surprising discoveries when you read the *Tsukuma War Chronicles* and other official histories. It is in this hope that I have written these pages.

Arrowroot

Some twenty years have passed since I traveled to the interior of Yoshino in Yamato. It was around 1912, at the end of the Meiji Period or the beginning of Taishō, when the transportation facilities that we have today were not available. And so I must begin my story by explaining what prompted me to set out for those mountain depths that have recently been dubbed the "Yamato Alps."

As some of my readers probably know, in the district around the Totsu River, Kitayama, and Kawakami Village legends survive concerning an heir to the Southern Court whom even today the inhabitants call the "Lord of the Southern Court" and the "Heavenly King." This Heavenly King, or Prince Kitayama, is said to have been a great-great-grandson of Emperor Gokameyama. He is not merely a legendary figure, but actually existed, as historians specializing in the period confirm. To give a brief summary: Most middle-school history texts explain that in 1392, during the time of the Shōgun Yoshimitsu, a reconciliation was accomplished and the rival courts merged, bringing an end to the Southern, Yoshino, Court fifty-seven years after it had been established by Emperor Godaigo. But late at night on the twenty-third of the Ninth Month, 1443, a certain Kusunoki Jirō Masahide, loyal to Prince Manjuji of the Southern line, launched a sudden attack on the

Tsuchimikado Palace; stole the three imperial regalia; and ensconced himself and his faction on Mount Hiei. They were attacked by a pursuing force from the capital, and Prince Manjuji took his own life; two of the regalia, the sword and the mirror, were recovered, but the jewel remained in the hands of the Southern adherents. Thereupon the Kusunoki and Ochi clans transferred their allegiance to Prince Manjuji's two sons and, raising a loyal army, fled to Ise, then to Kii and Yamato, and finally into the remote mountains of Yoshino, beyond the reach of the Northern Court's army. There they honored the elder prince as Heavenly King and his brother as shōgun, and chose the era name Tensei; for more than sixty years they guarded the sacred jewel in a canyon that the enemy would not easily find. It was in the Twelfth Month of 1457 that they were tricked by surviving retainers of the Akamatsu clan, the two princes killed, and the Southern line finally broken. For one hundred and twenty-two years, then—from 1336 to 1457—descendants of the Southern Court remained in Yoshino and opposed the capital faction.

As the residents of Yoshino have inherited a tradition of support for the Southern Court, it is natural that they should count its duration to the time of the Heavenly King. The Southern Court lasted, they insist, "not fifty-some years: it continued for more than a hundred." I, too, had been interested in the secret history of the Southern Court ever since reading the *Taiheiki* as a boy, and wanted to build a historical novel around the lingering traces of the Heavenly King.

According to a published collection of oral traditions from Kawakami Village, the surviving retainers of the Southern Court, fearing an attack from the Northern Court, moved from Shionoha, at the foot of Mount Ōdaigahara, to a canyon called Sannoko, deep in the little-known mountains toward Ōsugi Gorge, on the border of Ise Province. Here they built a palace for their lord and hid the sacred jewel in a cave. The *Kōtsuki Chronicle* and the *Akamatsu Chronicle* record that thirty refugees of the Akamatsu clan under Majima Hikotarō, having lied their way into the Southern Court, took advantage of a heavy snow on the second of the Twelfth Month, 1457, to make a surprise attack. One party struck at the King's Ōkōchi Palace as another moved on the Shōgun's palace in Kōno Valley. The Heavenly King defended himself with a longsword but was finally cut down by traitors, who escaped with his head and the sacred jewel. Impeded by the snow, however, they got only as far as Obagamine Pass before dark. There they buried the head in the snow and spent the night. The next morning they were attacked by officials from the eighteen villages of Yoshino. In the midst of the fighting, the King's head sent up a spurt of blood from beneath the snow, so that the villagers were able to recapture it.

The details of this incident vary somewhat from source to source, but there is no room for doubt: it also appears in *An Imperial Progress to the Southern Hills, Records of the South, The Blossom Cloud Chronicle* and the *Totsu River Chronicle*; moreover, the *Kōtsuki* and *Akamatsu* chronicles were written by veterans of the fighting, or their offspring. According to one book, the King was in his eighteenth year. The restoration of the House of Akamatsu, which had fallen in the Kakitsu Rebellion, was their reward for assassinating the two princes and restoring the sacred jewel to the capital.

Because of the inaccessibility of the area from the mountains of Yoshino to Kumano in the south, a number of old legends have been preserved, and families that have maintained their lineages over many generations are not uncommon. It is said, for example, that part of the Hori mansion in Anafu, where Emperor Godaigo once stayed, is still standing, occupied even now by descendants of the family. Also thriving are the progeny of Takehara Hachirō, who appears in "The Prince of the Great Pagoda Flees to Kumano," in the *Taiheiki*. The prince stayed with this family for a time and had a son by their daughter. An even older tradition survives in the hamlet of Gokitsugu, on Mount Ōdaigahara. Asserting that the people of Gokitsugu are descended from ogres, residents of the surrounding villages never marry them, and neither do the occupants themselves have any desire to marry outside the hamlet. They say they are descendants of the ogres who cleared the path for En-no-gyōja, the great ascetic. This being the nature of the region, there are a number of old families, called "people of descent," who claim to be descended from the local warriors who served the Southern Court. Even now they honor the "Lord of the Southern Court" every year, on February 5, with a majestic reenactment of the old New Year's ceremony at the Kongō Temple near Kashi-wagi, the site of the Shōgun-prince's palace in Kōno Valley. On this occasion, the "people of descent" are allowed to wear formal robes bearing the imperial chrysanthemum crest, and take precedence over the governor, the mayor, and other officials.

These various materials, as I became familiar with them, could only add to my enthusiasm for the historical novel I was planning. The Southern Court; the blossoms of Yoshino; the mysterious mountain recesses; the youthful King; Kusunoki Jirō Masahide; the sacred jewel, hidden deep in a cave; the head spouting blood through the snow— a writer could not hope for a more promising list of subjects. And the location was splendid. There were mountain streams, precipices, palaces and thatched roofs, cherry blossoms in the spring, and autumn foliage. Nor was it a groundless fantasy: official histories, of course, and chronicles and documents were available, all that one could desire, and a writer could produce an entertaining book simply by arranging properly the historical facts provided to him. And if he added a bit of decoration, wove in appropriate oral traditions and legends, peopled the landscape with some local figures—descendants of ogres, ascetics of Ōmine, pilgrims to Kumano—and created a beautiful heroine to go with the Heavenly King (a princess descended from the Prince of the Great Pagoda, perhaps), why, then it would be even more entertaining. I thought it odd that such a wealth of material had never attracted a writer's attention before. It is true that Bakin left an unfinished piece called "Biography of a Gallant," but I have not read it and, as it seems to concentrate on an imaginary Kusunoki lady named Koma, it probably has nothing to do with the history of the Heavenly King. Otherwise, there seem to be one or two works from the Tokugawa Period dealing with the Yoshino emperors, but it is doubtful how much they conform to historical facts. In short, I had never seen the subject treated in any of the usual forms, whether in fiction, in ballads, or on the stage, and I was determined to make use of the material before anyone else tried his hand at it.

At this point, however, through an unexpected connection, I was able to learn a great deal more about the geography and customs of these mountains. I had a college friend named Tsumura who, though from Osaka himself, had relatives living at Kuzu, in Yoshino; and through him I was able to inquire about the area.

There were two places called Kuzu on the Yoshino River. The name of the one downstream is written with the character for "arrowroot," while that upstream (where

Tsumura's relatives lived) is written "country nest." It is the latter which has been made famous by the nō play *Kuzu*, about Emperor Temmu.

But neither of the villages named Kuzu produces that arrowroot starch, or *kuzuko*, for which Yoshino is renowned. Most residents of the upper Kuzu live by making paper. They still employ a primitive method that is rarely seen elsewhere anymore, that of bleaching mulberry fibers in the waters of the Yoshino River and using them to make paper by hand. Tsumura's relatives, too, were engaged in papermaking—in fact, were the biggest producers in the village; their name was Kombu, an odd surname, but one extremely common where they lived. According to Tsumura, the Kombu were an old family who could probably count a few Southern Court survivors among their ancestors. It was from this family that I learned the correct readings of the characters for Shionoha and Sannoko. And it was the Kombu who told me that the distance from Kuzu to Shionoha was more than fifteen miles, across the treacherous Gosha Pass; and from there it was five miles to the mouth of Sannoko Canyon and another ten or more to the innermost point, where the Heavenly King is said to have lived. But they were only relaying to me what they had heard, for no one from Kuzu ever went that far upstream. A raftsman who came down the river said that deep in the canyon, in a basin called Hachiman Plain, was a hamlet of five or six charcoal makers; and that three or four miles farther on, at Hidden Plain in the head of the canyon, there were traces of the palace, as well as the cave where the sacred jewel had been enshrined. There was no path, however, for those ten miles beyond the mouth of the canyon, only a succession of sheer cliffs; and so even the Yamabushi ascetics of Mount Ōmine could scarcely penetrate that far. The people living around Kashiwagi usually went no farther than the hot springs bubbling up by the river at Shionoha. In fact, if one went deep into the canyon, one would find any number of hot springs welling from the middle of the stream, and countless waterfalls of great height, like Myōjin Falls; but this splendid scenery was known only to mountaineers and charcoal makers.

The raftsman's story enriched even further the world of my novel. The perfect detail, hot springs boiling from a mountain stream, was added to the promising items I had already assembled. But now I had completed my research on everything that could be investigated from a distance, and if Tsumura had not prodded me, I surely would never have set out for those mountain recesses. I had so much material that my imagination would take care of the rest, even without a visit to the site. In fact there are certain advantages to proceeding that way. But Tsumura wrote to me at the end of October or early in November that year. "Why don't you come along?" he urged. "You won't have a better opportunity than this." He had to call on his relatives in Kuzu, he said; I myself might not be able to go as far as Sannoko, but if I studied the topography and customs around Kuzu, I would surely learn much that would prove useful later. And there was more to the region than the history of the Southern Court. I would easily find enough local material on other subjects for two or three novels. Why not exercise my professional awareness to the full? I would not be wasting my time. And the season was perfect for travel. The cherry blossoms at Yoshino were proverbial, but the fall was lovely, too.

This has grown into a very long introduction; but it was under these circumstances that I abruptly decided to set out. Tsumura's "professional awareness" had something to do with it, but, to tell the truth, the prospect of a relaxed outing in the country was even more persuasive.

2 🐢 I M O S E Y A M A

Tsumura went from Osaka to Nara on the appointed day and took a room at an inn named Musashino, below Mount Wakakusa. I left Tokyo by night train, spent one night in Kyoto on the way, and arrived in Nara on the morning of the second day. There is still a Musashino Inn, but I am told that it is under different management now. Twenty years ago the building was old and, I thought, rather elegant. The Railroad Ministry had not built its hotel yet; the Musashino and the Kikusui were the best places to stay at the time. Tsumura looked as though he were tired of waiting, and I had seen the sights of Nara before, and so we decided to start right out before the weather changed. We rested for an hour or two gazing at Mount Wakakusa from the window of our room, then left the inn.

Changing at Yoshinoguchi, we took a rickety narrow-gauge train as far as Yoshino Station, and from there set off on foot along the highway that ran parallel to the Yoshino River. Near Mutsuda Pool and Willow Ford, familiar to readers of the *Man'yōshū* poems, the road divides in two. The right fork leads to the famous blossom sites of Mount Yoshino: crossing the river, one comes immediately to the groves of the Lower Thousand, then to the Sekiya cherries, Zaō Gongen Temple, Yoshimizu Temple, and the Middle Thousand, places that teem with cherry-blossom viewers every spring. I had come twice to see the blossoms at Yoshino, once as a child, when I accompanied my mother on an excursion to the Kyoto area, and once as a college student. And so I remembered going to the right and up the mountain road in a large group, but I had never taken the left fork before. Now that automobiles and cable cars go all the way to the Middle Thousand, no one lingers there anymore; but blossom viewers of earlier times, taking the right fork, would pause on the bridge at Mutsuda Pool and gaze at the scenery along the Yoshino River.

"There, please look there," the riksha man would say, pointing upstream from the railing on the bridge. "There you can see Imoseyama, the Wedded Hills, Imoyama on the left, Seyama on the right." My mother, too, had the riksha man stop in the middle of the bridge. Holding me, young and impressionable, on her lap, she whispered in my ear. "Do you remember the play about Imoseyama? Well, there is the real Imoseyama." I was very young, and the image is not clear in my mind; but the mountain air was still cold in the middle of April, and in the misty evening the Yoshino River flowed toward us under a pale, hazy sky, from a gap in the distant, overlapping mountains. Its rippled surface was like crepe in the path of the wind. Dimly, between the mountains, two small hills could be seen, rising abruptly through the evening mist. I could not make out the river flowing between them as they faced each other, but I knew from the theater that the hills were on opposite banks. On the kabuki stage, Koganosuke, the son of Daihanji Kiyozumi, and his betrothed, a maiden named Hinadori, live in mansions overlooking the valley, she on Imoyama and he on Seyama. That scene, of all in the Imoseyama play, is most like a fairy tale and, for that reason, made a strong impression on me as a child. When my mother spoke, I thought, "So that is Imoseyama," and indulged in the childish fantasy that, if I were to go there, I would meet Koganosuke and the maiden. The view from the bridge has stayed with me ever since. At unexpected moments I

recall it with a pang of nostalgia. And so when I came to
Yoshino the second time, in the spring of my twenty-first
or twenty-second year, I leaned once more on the bridge
railing and thought of my dead mother as I gazed upstream.
Here at the foot of Mount Yoshino the river enters a broad
plain, so that the tumbling stream begins to change into a
river that leisurely "through the mountainless country
flows." Upstream on the left bank I could see, clustered
along the highway, simple, rustic houses with low roofs and
mottled white walls. This was the town of Kamiichi, mountains at its back and the river before it.

This time I passed the foot of the bridge at Mutsuda and,
taking the left fork, went toward Imoseyama, a direction
in which I had only gazed from downstream before. The
highway extended in a straight line along the riverbank. It
appeared to be a flat, easy road; but I am told that from
Kamiichi it passes through Miyataki, Kuzu, Ōtaki, Sako,
and Kashiwagi, goes deep into the mountains of inner
Yoshino, reaches the source of the Yoshino River, crosses
the watershed between Yamato and Kii, and finally emerges
at Kumano Seashore.

Having left Nara early, we entered Kamiichi a little
past noon. The houses lining both sides of the highway
were, as I had imagined from the bridge, simple and old-
fashioned. There were occasional gaps between the houses
on the side toward the river, but for the most part the view
of the water was blocked. The houses on both sides had
lattices blackened by smoke, and low second stories,
scarcely more than attics. As I walked, I looked into the
shadows behind the lattices. As usual in country houses,
an earth-floored passage extended all the way to the back
door. At the entrance of most of these passages hung a dark-
blue curtain bearing in white the shop or family name. It
seemed to be customary for residences, as well as shops,

to have curtains. In every case the eaves drooped as though the façade had been crushed, and the frontage was narrow; but beyond the curtains, trees shimmered in courtyards and there was an occasional detached building. The houses were probably over fifty years old, some of them a hundred, or even two hundred. In contrast, the shoji paper on every house was new and spotless, as though it had just been changed, and the tiniest holes had been scrupulously covered with petal-shaped paper. The paper was a cold white in the clear autumn air. The lack of dust was one reason for this immaculacy, but another may have been that these people, because they do not use glass shoji, were more sensitive about their paper than city dwellers are. If there are no glass doors outside, as there are on houses in Tokyo, then the paper cannot be neglected, or it will get dirty and discolored; and the wind will blow in through the holes. The freshness of the shoji made the sooty lattices and furnishings in the rows of houses look neat and tasteful, like a beautiful woman who, though poor, is careful about her appearance. As I looked at the color of the sunlight shining on the paper, I felt the autumn deeply.

In fact, though the sky was dazzlingly clear, the light reflected there was bright but not glaring, and profoundly beautiful. The sun being over the river, it shone against the shoji on the left side of the street and was reflected deep into the houses on the right side. The persimmons displayed in front of a vegetable shop were particularly striking. Persimmons of all shapes—sweet persimmons, Gosho persimmons, Mino persimmons—caught the outdoor light on their glossy, ripe coral surfaces and glowed like eyes. Even the clumps of wheat noodles were bright inside a glass box at a noodle shop. On the street in front of the houses, cinders were spread out to air on straw mats and winnowing baskets. From somewhere came the sound of a blacksmith's hammer and the *sah-sah* of a rice polisher. We walked to the edge of town and had lunch at an eating house beside the river. When viewed from the bridge, Imoseyama had seemed much farther upstream, but here the two hills stood before our eyes. With the river between them, Imoyama was on this bank and Seyama on the other. This view, no doubt, gave the author of *Family Precepts for a Woman at Imoseyama* the idea for his play, but the river here is rather broad, not the narrow stream one sees on the stage. Even if the pavilions of Koganosuke and Hinadori were on the two hills, people would not have been able to call back and forth to each other as they do on stage. Seyama connects with the ridge behind and has an irregular shape, but Imoyama is a free-standing, conical hill, luxuriantly cloaked in green. The town of Kamiichi extends to the bottom of the hill. Seen from the river, the houses have an extra story in back, two-story houses becoming three, single-story houses becoming two. On some a cable runs from the upper floor to the river bottom. To this a bucket is attached, which is lowered by a rope to draw water.

"You know, after *Imoseyama* there is *Yoshitsune and the Thousand Cherry Trees*," said Tsumura abruptly.

"*The Thousand Cherry Trees* is set in Shimoichi, isn't it? I've heard of the Well Bucket Sushi Shop there. . . ." In the puppet play, Koremori is adopted by the owner of the sushi shop where he takes refuge. Though I had never been there, I had heard that some people in Shimoichi, inspired by this fiction, claimed to be his descendants. There is no Crooked Gonta in the family, they say, but the daughters are still named Osato, as in the play, and they make sushi in tubs resembling well buckets. But Tsumura was referring not to this part of the play but to Lady Shizuka's drum, Hatsune. There was a family upstream in the village of Natsumi who treasured the drum as an heirloom, and Tsumura proposed that we stop on the way to see it.

The village of Natsumi, I decided, would be on the banks of the Natsumi River mentioned in the nō play *Two Ladies Shizuka*: "To the shore of Natsumi River aimlessly a woman came. . . ." With these words, Shizuka's ghost appears. She says, "I am distressed by the weight of my sins, copy a sutra for me." Then, in the text of the dance that follows:

> *Truly am I ashamed,*
> *My heart cannot forget the past . . .*
> *Think not*
> *That you see now*
> *A woman picking greens*
> *From the River Natsumi*
> *In Yoshino.*

There would seem, then, to be some basis for the legends that associate Natsumi with Shizuka. *Famous Places in Yamato, Illustrated* says, "The village of Natsumi has excellent water, which is called flower-basket water. There is also the site of a mansion in which Lady Shizuka lived for a time"; and so the tradition is probably an old one. The family that had the drum went by the name Ōtani, but formerly had been known as the Murakuni stewards. According to old family records, it was said, Yoshitsune and Lady Shizuka stayed there when they fled to Yoshino in the 1180s. There were famous spots nearby—Kisa Brook, Napping Bridge, and Shiba Bridge—and sightseers sometimes asked to see the drum Hatsune; but because it was a family heirloom, it was not shown to casual visitors. One must have a proper introduction in advance. Accordingly, Tsumura had asked his relatives in Kuzu to make the arrangements, and so we were probably expected that day.

"When Lady Shizuka strikes the drum," I said, "a fox

appears, disguised as Tadanobu, because his parent's hide was used to make the drumheads. That's the one, isn't it?"

"Yes, that's how it is in the play."

"And the family says that they have the drum?"

"I've heard that they do."

"Is it really covered with fox skins?"

"That I can't promise, because I haven't seen it either. But there's no doubt that it's an old family."

"I wonder if this is not the same sort of thing as the Well Bucket Sushi Shop. A long time ago some wag probably invented it out of the nō play *Two Ladies Shizuka.*"

"Maybe, but I'm interested in that drum. I do want to visit the Ōtani house and see the drum Hatsune. I've wanted to for a long time, and that was one of the reasons for this trip."

So Tsumura said, and there seemed to be something behind it. But he added simply, "I'll tell you about it later," and said no more.

3 🎋 THE DRUM HATSUNE

From Kamiichi to Miyataki the road continued along the left bank of the Yoshino River. The autumn heightened as the mountains grew deeper. Again and again when we entered groves of oak trees, carpets of fallen leaves rustled under foot. The few maples were scattered, not in clusters; but the red leaves were at their peak: ivy, sumac, and lacquer trees dotted the cedar-covered peaks with every shade from the deepest crimson to the palest yellow. I said "red leaves," as people often do, but in fact there were complex varieties of yellow, brown, and red. Among the yellow leaves there were scores of different shades. It is said that everyone's face turns red in the fall at Shiohara in Shimotsuke. Foliage that is all one tint is a beautiful sight, but this kind is lovely too. There are elegant Chinese expressions to describe the riot of color in spring wild flowers, but here, too, with the difference that an autumn yellow set the tone, the variety of color was as rich as that of any field in spring. And through the light that spilled into the valleys from between the crags, the leaves fell, glittering like gold dust, to the water.

A number of spots mentioned in the *Man'yōshū*, including Emperor Temmu's villa at Yoshino, the "Grand Palace on the shore of the Yoshino rapids" of the poet Kasa no Kanamura, the Akizu fields of Hitomaro's poem, and Mount Mifune, are thought to have been near the present village of Miyataki. Before going very far into the village, we left the highway and crossed to the opposite bank. Here the valley gradually narrowed, the riverbanks became cliffs, and the seething water crashed against boulders in the riverbed and overflowed the pure blue pools. Kisa Brook, a murmuring stream that trickled from the wooded depths of Kisa Valley, was spanned by Napping Bridge where it emptied into a pool. The tradition that Yoshitsune napped at the bridge was probably the result of some later flight of imagination. The graceful, fragile-looking bridge spanning the rivulet of spring water was almost entirely hidden by a stand of trees, and the little roof may have been needed to protect the bridge more from leaves than from rain. It looked as though an uncovered bridge would quickly be buried in autumn leaves. There were two farmhouses on the approach to the bridge. The families apparently used the space under the roof for their own storage; the bridge was stacked with bundles of firewood, leaving just enough room for a person to pass. The place was called Higuchi. Here the road divided in two: one fork followed the river-bank to Natsumi Village, and the other crossed Napping Bridge, passed Sakuragi Shrine and Kisadani Village and led to the Upper Thousand, Koke-no-shimizu, and the poet Saigyō's hermitage. The man of Shizuka's poem, who "forged through the white snow on the peak," probably crossed the bridge and went from the inner mountains of Yoshino toward Chūin Valley.

When we finally took notice, the mountains ahead of us had become high and close. The sky narrowed, and the Yoshino River, the houses, and the road all looked as though they must arrive at a dead end in this canyon. But villages, it seems, will spread wherever there is an opening. On the slope of a cramped riverbank, in a basin like the inside of a sack, enclosed on three sides by mountain tem-pests, terraces had been cut, thatched roofs built, and fields planted. This was Natsumi Village. The river and the shape of the mountains did give it the look of a place where refugees from the capital might have lived.

We had no difficulty in finding the Ōtani house. It stood in a mulberry field, toward the river, about a third of a mile into the village. The roof was magnificent. The mulberries had grown so high that, from a distance, only the venerable thatch, with a sort of supplementary roof at the ridge and a tile roof at the eaves, could be seen floating above the leaves like an island on the sea. It looked most inviting. The house itself, however, was quite ordinary compared to the roof. A typical farmhouse, it had two adjoining rooms in front, facing the fields. The shoji were open, and in the room with the alcove sat the master of the house, a man of about forty. As soon as he saw us he came out to greet us, even before we could introduce ourselves. With his taut, sunburned face, tired, friendly eyes, small head, and broad shoulders, he was very much the simple, honest farmer. "I heard from Mr. Kombu in Kuzu, and I have been expecting you," he said, but even this simple welcome was spoken in a country dialect that I had difficulty understanding; and in response to our inquiries he only bowed formally without giving a clear reply. It occurred to me that the family had suffered a decline and retained little of its old prominence, but for me a man of this sort was more approachable. "We are sorry to trouble you when you are so busy. We have heard that you rarely show the family heirlooms, and it is rude of us to come like this to see them." "No, it's not that we don't want to show them. . . ." Shyly, and with a touch of embarrassment, he said that a family tradition required seven days of purification before the objects could be brought out; but the family could not very well observe such a fussy rule anymore, and would be happy to show the heirlooms to anyone who asked to see them, though, being busy with farm work, they did not have time to indulge unexpected callers. At this time of year, particularly, they were occupied with the autumn silkworms and, as a rule, the mats were taken up throughout the house. They would not even have a room in which to receive unexpected guests; but if one were kind enough to let him know in advance, he would always make arrangements and be waiting. He spoke haltingly; his hands, the fingernails quite black, rested formally on his knees.

It was clear, then, that he had relaid the mats in these two rooms in anticipation of our visit and had been waiting for us. Through a crack in the sliding doors I could see into the adjoining storeroom, where a jumble of farm tools had been piled hastily on the bare floorboards. The heirlooms were already set out in the alcove. Taking them one by one, the master reverently placed them before us: a scroll entitled "The History of Natsumi Village"; several long and short swords presented by Lord Yoshitsune; a catalogue of the gifts; sword guards; a quiver; a ceramic sake jar and the drum Hatsune, a gift from Lady Shizuka. The end of the scroll bore the inscription, "Written at the command of the visiting magistrate of Gojō, Naitō Mokuzaemon, by Ōtani Gembei, age seventy-six, as a record of what he had heard." It was dated "Summer 1855." There is a tradition that when the magistrate Naitō Mokuzaemon came to the village in 1855, the elderly Ōtani Gembei, forefather of the present head of the family, knelt in greeting; but when he presented this document, the magistrate gave him his seat and knelt before him. The scroll was, however, so dirty that it looked as though it were charred and, as it was difficult to read, a copy accompanied it. I do not know about the original, but the copy contained a great many errors in characters and syntax, and many of the readings were dubious; it was inconceivable that anyone with a formal education had written it. According to the text, the family ancestors had lived on this site since the Nara Period; in the succession war of 672, the Murakuni steward Oyori had supported Emperor Temmu and killed Emperor Kōbun. In those days, it said, the steward governed the three and a half miles from this village to Kamiichi, and so "Natsumi River" referred to that portion of the Yoshino River. There was this on Yoshitsune: "Lord Minamoto Yoshitsune celebrated the Festival of the Fifth Month at Mount Shiraya in Kawakami, then descended and stayed in the house of the Murakuni steward for thirty or forty days. When he saw Shiba Bridge at Miyataki, he composed these verses," and two poems are given. To this day I do not know of any poems by Yoshitsune. Even to an untrained eye the two poems recorded there were not in the style of the late Heian Period, and the diction was vulgar. Next, concerning Lady Shizuka: "At that time Lord Yoshitsune's beloved mistress Lady Shizuka was staying in the Murakuni house. After Lord Yoshitsune fled to Mutsu, she lost all hope and threw herself into a well. It is called Shizuka's Well." According to the scroll, then, she died here. Further, "Yet Lady Shizuka, perhaps distracted by her separation from Lord Yoshitsune, rose as a spirit fire from the well every night for three hundred years. At that time, the holy man Rennyo was in the village of Iigai leading everyone to the Buddha, and the village people begged him to work salvation for Shizuka's ghost. Without hesitation the holy man led her to the Buddha, then wrote a poem on the sleeve of Lady Shizuka's robe, which was in the keeping of the Ōtani family." The poem was included. As we read the scroll, our host sat quietly, offering no word of explanation. But the expression on his face suggested that he accepted without question the accounts handed down from his ancestor. "What happened to the robe, on which the holy man wrote his poem?" we asked. He replied that his forebears had given it to a village temple called Saishōji, as a prayer for Shizuka's rebirth in paradise, but no one knew where it had gone, and the temple did not have it. The swords and the quiver, when we picked them up and examined them, appeared to be very old, the quiver in particular being badly damaged and worn, but they were not things we could appraise. As for the drum Hatsune—there was no skin, only the shell stored in a paulownia-wood box. We could not be sure about the drum either, but the lacquer seemed relatively new, and there was no ornamentation; to all appearances, it was a thoroughly unexceptional, solid black shell. The wood, however, did look old, and so perhaps it had been relacquered at some point. "Yes, maybe it was," our host replied indifferently.

There were also two imposing memorial tablets, equipped with roofs and doors. On the door of one was a mallow-leaf crest, and inside the inscription "Tablet of the Prime Minister of the First Rank, Senior Grade." The other had an apricot-blossom crest on the door, and the inscription inside read, "Toward Nirvana. Tablet of Shōyo-teigyoku," which was apparently the posthumous name of a lady. On the right side was "The Second Year of Gembun," corresponding to 1737, and on the left, "Eleventh Month, Tenth Day." Our host, however, knew nothing about the tablets. From ancient times it had been said that they commemorated the Ōtani family's lord, and it was a family custom to do reverence to the tablets on the first of every year. The one with the Gembun date, he added, gravely, might be that of Lady Shizuka.

His gentle, timid, tired eyes kept us from saying anything. There was no point in telling him when the Gembun Period was, or in citing the *Mirror of the East* or the *Tale of the Heike* on the life of Lady Shizuka. The master of the house believed it all implicitly. And the lady that he imagined was not necessarily the same Shizuka who danced before Yoritomo at the Tsurugaoka Shrine. For him she was a noblewoman who symbolized the days of his distant ancestors, the cherished past. The phantom aristocrat called "Lady Shizuka" was the focus of his reverence and devotion for "ancestors," "lord," and "antiquity." There was no need to question whether the noble lady had actually sought lodging in this house and lived here in loneliness. It was best to leave him with the beliefs that were so important to him. And if we take a sympathetic view, perhaps when the family was in its prime there was an incident involving, if not Shizuka herself, a princess from the Southern Court or a refugee of the civil wars of the sixteenth century, and this incident became intertwined with the Shizuka legend.

As we were about to take our leave, the master of the house said, "We don't have much to offer, but please try some ripers." He made tea and brought out a bowl of persimmons with a clean, empty fire tray.

"Ripers" apparently means "ripe persimmons." The empty fire tray was to be used not as an ashtray, but as a dish from which to eat the soft, ripe persimmons. Following his urgings, I carefully put one of them on the palm of my hand. It looked as though it might burst at any moment. A large, conical persimmon with a pointed bottom, it had ripened to a deep, translucent red, and though swollen like a rubber bag, it was as beautiful as jade when held up to the light. The cask-sweetened persimmons that are sold in the city never achieve this fine color, however ripe they become, and they fall apart before they get this soft. Our host said that only thick-skinned Mino persimmons were suitable for making ripers. They are picked while still hard and sour and are put away where no breeze will strike them, in boxes or baskets. In ten days, without any human interference, the insides naturally turn to semiliquid as sweet as nectar. Other persimmons will get watery, not viscous like the Mino variety. By removing the stem and eating through the hole with a spoon, one can eat them like soft-boiled eggs; but they taste better if they are placed in a dish, peeled, and eaten by hand, though this method is rather messy. Just ten days will bring them to their most beautiful and delicious stage, but any longer than that will turn ripers into water.

As I listened to this account, I gazed at the pearl of dew in my hand. It was as though the mystery and the sunshine of the mountains had congealed on my palm. I have heard that country people visiting the capital used to take packets of soil home with them as mementos; and if someone were to ask me about the color of the autumn at Yoshino, I think I would take some of these persimmons home to show.

In the end, what impressed me most at the Ōtani house were the ripers, not the drum or the documents. Tsumura and I each devoured two of the sweet, syrupy persimmons, reveling in the penetrating coolness from our gums to our intestines. I filled my mouth with the Yoshino autumn. Even the mangoes of the Buddhist texts may not have tasted as good.

4 ❧ THE CRY OF THE FOX

"The history scroll said only that the drum Hatsune was a relic of Lady Shizuka; there was nothing about fox skins."

"That's right. But I think that the drum predates the play. If the play had come first, the drum would have been made to have more connection with the plot. Just as the author of *Imoseyama* got his idea from seeing the actual scene, the author of *The Thousand Cherry Trees* must have visited the Ōtani house, or heard about it, and developed his ideas from there. The only problem is that the author of *The Thousand Cherry Trees* is Takeda Izumo, and so the play had to have been written before the seventeen-fifties; but the history scroll was written in eighteen-fifty-five. Still, the tradition must be older than that, because the scroll said that it was 'written by Ōtani Gembei, age seventy-six, as a record of what he had heard.' Even if the drum is a fake, I think it's reasonable to suppose that it was there long before eighteen-fifty-five. Wouldn't you think so?"

"But the drum looked new, didn't it?"

"Oh, yes, perhaps it is new. But I believe that there have been two or three generations of drums, each one relacquered and rebuilt. Before the drum we saw, there were other, older ones in that paulownia box."

The famous Shiba Bridge led from Natsumi back to Miyataki on the opposite bank. We sat down on the rocks at the foot of the bridge and talked for a while.

In *A Tour of Yamato*, Kaibara Ekiken writes, "Miyataki is not a waterfall, as the name suggests. There are great rocks on both sides. The Yoshino River flows between them. Both banks consist of gigantic rocks, about thirty feet high, erect like folding screens. Between the banks the river is about twenty feet wide. At the narrowest point there is a bridge. Because the river narrows when it reaches here, the water is very deep and the view superb." This describes the view from the rocks where we were resting. "Villagers called rock jumpers leap from the rocks into the water and swim downstream, where they emerge. They collect money for this performance. When they jump, they keep their hands at their sides and their feet together. Entering the water to a depth of about ten feet, they rise to the surface by extending their arms." There is a picture of the rock jumpers in *Famous Places Illustrated*, and the shape of the banks and the course of the stream are just as they are shown in the illustration. The river makes a sharp curve here as it plunges, foaming between the crags. Mr. Ōtani had told us that it was not uncommon for rafts to break up against these rocks. And the rock-jumping villagers had spent their time fishing and plowing. When travelers came along, they would solicit money and perform their feat. They charged one hundred coppers to jump from the opposite bank, where the rocks were somewhat lower, and two hundred to jump from a high rock on this side. This was why one was called Hundred Copper Rock, and the other, Two Hundred Copper Rock. The names persist even now; but recently there were fewer travelers, Mr. Ōtani said, and the practice had died out, though he had seen it in his youth.

"Most people who came to see the blossoms in the old days, before the railroad was built, traveled by way of Uda County and passed here. In other words, the route that Yoshitsune took when he escaped from the capital must have been the usual course. Surely Takeda Izumo came here, too, and saw the drum Hatsune." For some reason Tsumura was still thinking about Hatsune as he sat on the rocks. He was not fox-Tadanobu, he said, but he was drawn to the drum even more than the fox had been. When he saw it he felt as though he were meeting his own parent.

At this point, I must tell you something more about Tsumura. I did not know the details myself until he confided in me there on the rocks. As I said before, we had been classmates in college, and rather intimate, but when it came time to go from college to the university, he went home to Osaka, for family reasons, and gave up his studies. He told me at the time that his family had been pawnbrokers for generations in the Shimanouchi district of Osaka. His parents died early, and he and his two sisters were reared by their grandmother. The older sister had been married for some time, and now his younger sister, too, was engaged to be married. His grandmother was feeling lonely, there was no one to look after the family business, and so he decided abruptly to leave school. I urged him to go to Kyoto University, but he said that he was more interested in writing than in studying; the business could be left to the clerk, while he would be happiest to write fiction in his spare time.

We corresponded occasionally after that, but there were

no indications that he was writing anything but letters. Ambition is bound to wane when a young man settles down to a carefree life at home, and Tsumura, too, as he got used to his situation, probably was content with the tranquil life of a merchant. Two years later, when I read in the margin of one of his letters that his grandmother had died, I supposed that he would soon find an elegant young bride in the Osaka mold and become a thorough Shimanouchi gentleman.

Subsequently Tsumura visited Tokyo two or three times, but this outing was our first opportunity to have a good talk since he left school. Meeting my friend after a long separation, I found that he looked much as I had expected him to. Both men and women change physically when they leave school and settle down at home, their skin getting whiter and their bodies fuller, as though their diet had suddenly improved. In Tsumura's case, his personality, too, had developed the quiet affability of a pampered young man from Osaka, and his accent (even stronger now than before) blended with lingering traces of student language. This, then, should be enough to suggest Tsumura's outward appearance.

As for Tsumura's affinity with the drum Hatsune, which he began suddenly to explain to me there on the rocks, his motives for planning the trip, and his secret objective—it is a rather long story, but I will repeat what he told me as briefly as possible.

It may be (he began) that only a fellow Osakan who has lost his parents early, as I did, and cannot remember their faces, will understand how I feel. As you know, three kinds of music are native to Osaka, the *jōruri* ballads, koto compositions of the Ikuta School, and *jiuta* songs. I am not a

music lover, but these forms of music were part of my surroundings. I often heard them and have been unconsciously
affected by them. I especially remember a scene in an inner
room of the Shimanouchi house, when I was four or five
years old. A refined townswoman with a pale complexion
and bright, clear eyes was playing the koto, accompanied
by a blind shamisen master. I think that the image of the
woman playing the koto is the only trace of my mother that
remains in my memory; but it is not certain that the lady
was in fact my mother. Years later, my grandmother told
me that the lady had probably been herself, that my mother
had died a little before that. Strangely, though, I remember that the master and the lady were playing an Ikuta
piece called "Konkai," or "The Cry of the Fox." Because
my grandmother and both of my sisters were students of
the same master, I heard "The Cry of the Fox" many times
thereafter, and the image was constantly refreshed. These
are the lyrics:

> *Oh, how sad, how sad*
> *Mother unlike a flower*
> *In the bed of fading dew*
> *The mirror of wisdom*
> *Clouds over.*
> *Meeting a priest*
> *Mother turns*
> *When I beckon*
> *As if to say farewell.*
> *There is nothing but to cry.*
> *Across the fields and across the hills*
> *Passing through the villages*
> *For whom do you come? For thee.*
> *For whom do you come, for whom?*
> *I come for thee.*

Are you leaving? Oh, the pain.
To the forest where I dwell
I shall return
In my longing heart
My longing heart unknowing
Through white chrysanthemums
Through the rocks and through the ivy,
Forging through
The narrow bamboo path,
Lovely are the voices
Of the insects.
It begins to rain, oh
It begins to rain,
Even this morning
Even this morning
No trace remains
In the western fields
The levees are precarious,
Cross with faltering steps
The valleys and the peaks,
Cross over that hill
Cross over this hill,
Yearning, yearning, languishing.

Since then I have learned the melody and the instrumental interludes, as well; but something in the lyrics must have gone straight to my young impressionable heart, for me to remember hearing the piece being played by the master and the woman.

Jiuta lyrics are full of incoherent, grammatically confused passages, and the obscurity often seems to be deliberate. Songs that draw upon traditions from the nō theater or from *jōruri* are particularly difficult to understand without a knowledge of the sources, and "The Cry of the Fox" is probably of this kind. Yet the lines, "Oh, how sad, how sad / Mother unlike a flower" and "Mother turns / When I beckon / As if to say farewell," are filled with the grief of a boy who yearns for his fleeing mother, and somehow made an impression on me as an innocent child. "Across the fields and across the hills / Passing through the villages," and "Cross over that hill / Cross over this hill," sound a bit like a lullaby. I had no way of knowing what the characters for "Konkai" meant; but gradually, as I heard the song again and again, I became vaguely aware that it had something to do with a fox.

This was probably because I was often taken by my grandmother to see puppet plays at the Bunraku and Horie theaters, and the scene in *Arrowroot Leaves*, in which the mother parts from her son, made a deep impression on me. The rhythmic sound of the reed, as the fox-mother weaves in an autumn evening; the poem she writes on the shoji, her heart heavy because she has to leave her sleeping child behind:

> *If you miss me*
> *Come and search*
> *Shinoda Forest*
> *In Izumi . . .*

—the power of these scenes to move a boy who did not know his mother would be difficult for someone in other circumstances to imagine. In the lines, "My longing heart / My longing heart unknowing / Through white chrysanthemums / Through the rocks and through the ivy / Forging through / The narrow bamboo path," the child of the song desperately chases the retreating figure of the white fox as she runs along the colorful autumn path toward her den in the forest; putting myself in this child's place, I felt the absence of my mother all the more keenly.

Perhaps because Shinoda Forest is near Osaka, songs about the fox-mother are often a part of the games that children play at home. I remember two; one of them is:

> *Let us catch her, let us catch her*
> *The fox of Shinoda Forest*
> *Let us catch her.*

As the children sing, one plays the fox and two others are hunters, who hold a large loop of string between them with which to catch the fox. Hearing that there was a similar game in Tokyo, I once asked some geisha to play it for me at a teahouse; but the words and melody are somewhat different from the Osaka version. And in Tokyo the players remain seated. In Osaka they play standing up, and the "fox" gradually approaches the loop, cavorting in fox movements in time to the music. This is particularly charming when the "fox" is a pretty girl, or a young bride. I still remember one January evening; I had been invited to play at a relative's house, and there I saw an ingenuous and very beautiful young woman whose fox imitation was amazingly skillful. Now, in the other game, a number of children sit in a circle holding hands, with "it" seated in the middle. As the children sing, they pass a small object, such as a bean, from hand to hand so that "it" cannot see it. When the song ends, everyone freezes and "it" tries to guess whose hand holds the bean. Here are the words to that song:

> *Picking barley*
> *Picking wormwood*
> *In our hands are nine beans*
> *Nine beans, but more than that*

Arrowroot

We miss our parents' home—
If you miss me
Come and search
Shinoda Forest's arrowroot leaves of sorrow.

I sense a child's homesickness in this song, if only faintly. Many youngsters come from the countryside of Kawachi and Izumi to work in Osaka shops as articled apprentices and maidservants. On cold winter nights in the tradesmen's houses of Semba and Shimanouchi, you can see these servants lock the front door and join the family around the brazier to sing this song. It seems to me now that when those children, who had left their back-country villages to learn about commerce and good manners, sang "We miss our parents' home," they must have thought about their fathers and mothers lying in the dimly lit rooms of thatched-roof houses. Later, I heard the song used for musical accompaniment in the sixth act of *The Faithful Retainers*, when the two samurai come calling, their faces hidden in deep basket hats; and I was impressed at how well matched the song was to the plight of Yoichibei, Okaya, and Okaru.

There were many young servants in the house at Shimanouchi. When I saw them play, singing this song, I was both sympathetic and envious. They had left their fathers and mothers to live with strangers, and this was sad; yet they had parents whom they could see anytime simply by going home. I did not have. This gave me the idea that I could meet my mother if I went to Shinoda Forest, and in the second or third grade of primary school I slipped away from home and went there with a classmate. Even now it is a rather inaccessible place, a mile-and-a-half walk from a stop on the Nankai Electric line, and at the time there may not even have been a train, for I seem to remember riding in a broken-down stagecoach and walking a good distance. In a forest of giant camphor trees, I found the Arrowroot Leaf Shrine of Inari, the harvest god, and a well called the Looking Glass of the Arrowroot Leaf Princess. I was comforted a little by the pictures in the votive hall— tablets depicting the scene in which the fox-mother leaves her son, and a portrait of the actor Jakuemon. Then, along the road that led me away from the forest, I listened fondly to the familiar clack, clack of looms, coming from behind the shoji of the farmhouses. The road passed through the area where Kawachi cotton is produced, and there must have been many weavers. The sound went a long way toward soothing my unhappiness.

Yet it seems strange that I missed my mother so much, and not my father, for my father died first. And it is possible that the image of my mother lingers somewhere in my memory, but my father's could not. This suggests to me that the love for my mother was simply a vague yearning for the "unknown woman," in other words, that it was connected with the first buddings of adolescent love. In my case, the woman of the past who was my mother, and the woman who will be my wife in the future, are both "unknown women," and both are tied to me by an invisible thread of fate. This state of mind is probably latent in everyone to a certain extent, even in those whose circumstances are different from my own. There is evidence of this in "The Cry of the Fox." Lines such as "For whom do you come? I come for thee" and "Are you leaving? Oh, the pain" suggest a child's longing for his mother, but also sound like the anguish of a lovers' parting. No doubt the author of the song deliberately made the lyrics vague enough to permit both interpretations. At all events, I am convinced that, from the first time I heard the song, my imagination saw more than just my mother. The figure I saw was my mother, I think, and at the same time, my wife.

And so the image of my mother that I held in my little breast was not that of a matron, but that of an eternally young and beautiful woman. The mother of my dreams was like the mother of the packhorse driver Sankichi on the stage—the splendid noblewoman Shigenoi, wearing a magnificent robe and serving as nursemaid to a daimyo's daughter; and in my dreams, I was Sankichi.

It may be that the playwrights of the Tokugawa Period were surprisingly clever at playing upon the subconscious of their audiences. In the play about Sankichi, a princess is placed on one side and a packhorse boy on the other, with the lady-in-waiting, who is both wet nurse and mother, between them. On the surface, the play deals with the love of parents and children, but in the shadows, a boy's still undefined romantic feelings are suggested. From Sankichi's point of view, at least, his mother and the princess, living in the daimyo's stately inner palace, both could be the objects of his longing. In *Arrowroot Leaves*, the father and the son are of one mind in their love for the mother; but in this case the spectators' fantasies are sweetened by the device of making the mother a fox. I always wished that my mother were a fox, as in the play, and I envied the little boy terribly. For I could never hope to meet my mother in this life, because she was human; but if she were a fox in human form, who could say that she might not again appear as my mother someday? Surely any motherless child seeing the play would feel the same. In the journey-dance of *The Thousand Cherry Trees*, the imaginative association of mother, fox, beautiful woman, and lover is more intimate still. Both parent and child are foxes and, while Shizuka and fox-Tadanobu are depicted as mistress and vassal, the scene is contrived to look like a lovers' journey. Perhaps that is why this dance-play was my favorite. I likened myself to fox-Tadanobu. In my imagination I was lured on by the sound of the drum on which my parent's skin was stretched, and followed Lady Shizuka through the cherry-blossom clouds of Mount Yoshino. I even thought of studying dance, so that I could be Tadanobu on the recital stage.

"But that's not all," he added, gazing across the river to the forest shadows of Natsumi Village. Night was coming on. "This time I feel as though I have actually been drawn to Yoshino by the drum Hatsune." And a smile, the meaning of which I did not understand, came to his good-natured eyes.

5   K U Z U

From here on I shall present Tsumura's account indirectly.

The special fondness that Tsumura felt for the Yoshino region was partly due, then, to the influence of *The Thousand Cherry Trees*. The other reason for it was the knowledge that his mother had come from the province of Yamato. Exactly where in Yamato she had come from, and whether her family survived, were matters that remained cloaked in mystery for a long time. He questioned his grandmother, wanting to learn as much as possible while she was still alive, but he was unable to elicit any clear answers: she said only that she could not remember. Strangely, none of his aunts and uncles knew where his mother had come from, either. Because the Tsumura were an old family, a relationship of two or three generations would have been a matter of course under normal circumstances. But the fact was that Tsumura's mother had not come directly from Yamato to marry his father; she had been sold as a child into one of the Osaka pleasure districts, and then been adopted by a respectable family before her marriage. According to the entries in the family register, then, she was born in 1863; was given in marriage by Urakado Yoshijūrō, of Number 3 Imabashi, in 1877, at the age of fourteen; and died in 1891 at the age of twenty-eight. This is all that Tsumura had been able to learn about his mother by the time he graduated from middle school. Later he realized that his grandmother and other family elders had not been forthcoming because they did not like to talk about his mother's past. But to Tsumura, the fact that his mother had grown up in the demimonde served only to increase his longing; he did not find it particularly dishonorable or disagreeable. This was all the more so because she had married at fourteen; and even in that age of early marriages, she probably remained a pure young girl, scarcely touched by the sordidness of her society. It was by virtue of this, no doubt, that she had borne three children. Brought to her husband's house as an unsophisticated girl, she must have been instructed in the various accomplishments befitting the mistress of an old family. Tsumura had once seen a koto practice book that his mother had copied at the age of sixteen or seventeen. On a large piece of paper, folded into four, she had written the lyrics horizontally and, between the lines, carefully added the koto notation in red ink. It was in a beautiful hand, in the Oie style of calligraphy.

After that, Tsumura went to Tokyo for school and naturally grew away from his family, but his desire to find his mother's home only increased. In fact, it would be no exaggeration to say that his youth was spent in yearning for his mother. He felt a slight curiosity about the streetwalkers, young ladies, geisha, and actresses he passed on the street, it is true; but the women who caught his attention were always those whose faces somehow resembled the image of his mother that he knew from photographs. When he decided to leave school and return to Osaka, it was not only because his grandmother wished him to do so, but also because he was drawn to the region—to a spot a little nearer his mother's hometown, and to the house in Shimanouchi where she had spent half of her short life. There was also the fact that his mother was a woman of western Japan. In Tokyo he rarely met a woman who resembled her, but in Osaka he occasionally would. He had heard only that she had grown up in a pleasure quarter and, to his regret, he did not know exactly where; but in order to meet a vision of his mother, he associated with courtesans and drank at the teahouses. As a consequence, he fell secretly in love more than once. He won a reputation for dissipation. But because his activity arose simply from a longing for his mother, he never went too far, and preserved his chastity. Then, after three years, his grandmother died.

Shortly after her death, he set about putting her things in order. He began by going through a chest of drawers in the storehouse. Mixed in with papers in his grandmother's hand were some old documents and letters that he had never seen before. They included love letters exchanged by his parents while his mother was still indentured; a letter addressed to his mother, apparently from her mother in Yamato Province; and certificates from her koto, shamisen, flower-arranging, and tea-ceremony instructors. The love letters—three from his father and two from his mother —were no more than the childish intimacies of a youth and a girl in the ecstasy of first love, but they demonstrated the precocity of young people in those days: apparently the

couple had been meeting in secret, and, though the callig-
raphy was immature, the elegant, classical language of his
mother's letters was quite polished for a girl of fourteen.
From her family in the country there was only one letter.
It was addressed to "Miss Sumi, care of Mr. Konakawa,
Number 9, Shimmachi, Osaka City," and was from "Kombu
Sukezaemon family, Kubokaito, Kuzu Village, Yoshino
County, Yamato Province." The letter began: "I am writing because we are so grateful to you for being such a devoted child. The air grows colder with every passing day,
but we are relieved to know that you are getting on well.
Your papa and I thank you from the bottom of our hearts."
This was followed by a long list of injunctions: she must
think of the master of the house as her parent, and be
devoted to him; practice her lessons intently; not covet
things that belong to others; have faith in the gods and
buddhas; and so on. Seated on the dusty floor of the storehouse, Tsumura read the letter over and over in the failing
light. Finally, when he realized that the sun had gone down,
he went to his study and spread out the letter under an
electric lamp. Floating above the paper was the image of
the old woman, hunched over in the light of an oil lamp in
a farmhouse in Kuzu, rubbing the gum from her eyes as
she composed this letter to her daughter. It was a scroll,
more than twelve feet long. There were some doubtful
points in spelling and phrasing, as one would expect in the
letter of a country grandmother, but the characters were
abbreviated correctly in the Oie style: it was a good hand,
and not that of a simple peasant. Clearly, though, some
trouble had come to their lives and they had exchanged
their daughter for money. The letter was dated December
7; unfortunately, the year was not indicated, but there was
reason to guess that it was the first letter she had written

to her daughter after sending her to Osaka. Yet some passages hinted at the loneliness of one who did not have many years to live: "This is your mama's last testament," and, "Even when there is no life in me any longer, I will always be with you, helping you to succeed." Particularly interesting among the anxious warnings, not to do this, not to do that, was a lengthy admonition not to waste paper. "This paper was made by your mama and Orito. Always keep it next to your heart and cherish it. You may live in luxury and want for nothing, but you must not waste paper. Your mama and Orito worked hard to make this paper. Our hands are chapped and cracked and the tips of our fingers torn." Altogether, this exhortation filled twenty lines. From it, Tsumura learned that his mother's relatives had been papermakers and that there was a woman, apparently his mother's sister, named Orito. A woman named Oei also appeared. "Oei goes every day into the mountains, where the snow is deep, to dig arrowroot. We are all working to save money and when we have enough to pay the fares, we will visit you. You can look forward to that." The letter ended with a poem:

> The heart of a parent
> Who sighs for her child is benighted—
> And that is why I long
> For Darkness Pass.

Before the days of the railroad, "Darkness Pass" was crossed by everyone who took the old highway from Osaka to Yamato. The temple at the summit of the pass was famous as a place to listen to cuckoos, and Tsumura had gone there in middle school. Ascending the mountain one night, he had stopped to rest at the temple. Around four or five

o'clock in the morning, as the outside of the shoji began
to whiten faintly, a cuckoo suddenly called once from the
hills behind his room. Then there was another call, whether
from the same bird or a different one, and then another.
Presently the cuckoos were singing so much that there was
no longer any novelty in it. Tsumura took the cuckoos for
granted at the time, but when he read this poem, he recalled their cries with the greatest nostalgia. He thought he
understood why the ancients had compared this bird's song
to the souls of the dead.

But it was elsewhere in the old woman's letter that Tsumura felt the strangest affinity. His maternal grandmother
expounded repeatedly on foxes. "Every morning of every
day from now on you must pray to the shrine of Lord
Inari and to the white fox, Myōbu-no-shin. As you know,
the fox always comes when your papa calls. This is because
we are all of one heart." "I know that we were able to overcome our recent difficulties only with the help of the white
fox. Every day I pray for the health and good fortune of
the people you are with. We must have faith." It was clear
from passages like these that Tsumura's grandparents were
devout worshippers of Inari. "The shrine of Lord Inari"
was presumably a small shrine built inside the house, and
Inari's messenger, the white fox named "Myōbu-no-shin,"
probably had a den nearby. As for "The fox always
comes when your papa calls," it was not clear whether the
white fox actually came out of his hole in response to the
old man's voice, or entered the old woman or the old man
himself as a spirit possession. But Tsumura's grandfather
could summon the fox at will; and the fox, in attendance
on the old couple, controlled the destiny of the entire
family.

"This paper was made by your mama and Orito. Always
keep it next to your heart and cherish it," the letter said.

Tsumura pressed the scroll to his heart reverently. If the letter was sent to Tsumura's mother soon after she had been sold to Osaka, or before 1877, then it was thirty or forty years old; but the paper, though aged to a beautiful brown, was of finer texture than modern paper, and very sturdy. Tsumura held it to the light and examined the strong, thin fibers. He recalled the lines, "Your mama and Orito worked hard to make this paper. Our hands are chapped and cracked and the tips of our fingers torn." He sensed that the paper, which was not unlike an old woman's skin, held the blood of the woman who had borne his mother. No doubt his mother, too, when the letter arrived at the house in Shimmachi, had pressed it reverently to her heart as he had done; and so, "Bearing the fragrance of the sleeves / Of the one of old," the letter was a doubly sweet and precious remembrance.

Subsequently, Tsumura used the clues provided by the letter to locate his mother's family. There is no need to describe the process in detail. The period thirty or forty years before had seen the upheavals attendant upon the Meiji Restoration. The Konakawa house at Number 9, Shimmachi, into which his mother had been sold, and the Urakado family of Imabashi, by whom she had been adopted shortly before her marriage, were both gone; and the family lines of the tea, flower, koto, and shamisen masters who had signed her certificates had died out. The letter, then, was his sole lead; and the easiest, indeed the only, approach was to visit the village of Kuzu in Yoshino County, Yamato Province. In the winter of the year that his grandmother died, Tsumura observed the hundred-day services, and then, confiding his true purpose to no one, set off resolutely for Kuzu.

The changes in the countryside would have been less dramatic than in Osaka. And Kuzu was particularly out-

of-the-way, almost a cul-de-sac in the mountains of Yoshino County. Even a poor farm family would not have
disappeared entirely in the space of two or three generations. Excited by this prospect, Tsumura hired a ricksha in
Kamiichi one bright December morning, and hurried toward Kuzu by the highway along which he and I had
walked today. When he caught his first eager glimpse of
the village houses, his eyes were immediately drawn to the
paper set out to dry under the eaves of nearly every house.
Arranged on boards, the rectangular sheets of paper stood
in neat rows, just as seaweed is set out to dry in fishing
villages. Scattered like huge cards on both sides of the highway, on the terraced hillside, high and low, the pure-white
paper sparkled in the cold sunlight. Tears came to Tsumura's eyes. This was the land of his forebears. He had
long dreamed of his mother's home; now he set foot on the
very soil of it. When his mother was born, this timeless
mountain village had no doubt presented the same peaceful
scene that he saw now. Forty years ago the days passed just
as they did now. Tsumura felt as though he were right next
door to the past. If he closed his eyes for a moment, he
might see his mother when he opened them, playing with a
group of little girls inside the rough bamboo fence nearby.

"Kombu" being an unusual name, he had expected to
locate the family quickly, but when he arrived at the neighborhood called Kubokaito he learned that there were a
great many families named Kombu. There was nothing to
do but go with the ricksha man from door to door, asking
at each Kombu household. Maybe in the old days, he was
told, but there was no one today named Kombu Sukezaemon. At length a village elder emerged from the back of a
sweetshop. "That may be the one you're looking for."
Standing on the verandah, he pointed to a thatched roof

on the hillside to the left of the highway. Tsumura asked the ricksha man to wait at the sweetshop and, leaving the road, followed a gradually steepening path about sixty yards up an easy slope, toward the thatched roof. The morning was cold, but three or four houses were grouped in a congenial pocket of sunlight, sheltered from the wind, with a gently sloping hill behind them. Paper was being made at each house. As he went up the path, Tsumura realized that some young women in the houses above were pausing in their work to look down curiously at the unfamiliar young city gentleman coming toward them. Papermaking appeared to be the job of girls and young women; working in the open spaces in front of the houses, most of them wore hand towels tied around their heads. Through the clear, invigorating light that reflected from the paper and the towels, Tsumura approached the house that had been pointed out to him. The nameplate said "Kombu Yoshimatsu," not Sukezaemon. To the right of the main house was a shed with a plank floor, on which a girl of seventeen or eighteen squatted with her hands immersed in water that was as cloudy as though rice had been washed in it. She moved a wooden frame back and forth in the water, then raised it smartly. As the white water in the frame ran through the bottom, which was woven like a steaming basket, it deposited there a sheet of sediment the shape of a piece of paper. Transferring this sheet to its place in a row on the plank floor, the girl once again plunged the frame into the water. The front door of the shed being open, Tsumura stood behind a hedge of faded chrysanthemums and watched as the girl expertly made two, then three, sheets of paper. She was slender but, very much the country girl, solidly built and had a large frame. Her cheeks were firm and had the healthy luster of youth;

but Tsumura's heart was drawn to her fingers, immersed in the cloudy water. No wonder their hands were "chapped and cracked and the tips of our fingers torn." But even her fingers, red, swollen, and raw in the cold air, had a youthful vigor that was not to be suppressed. There was a sort of pathetic beauty in them.

When he shifted his attention, he caught sight of an old Inari shrine at the left corner of the main house. Tsumura's feet led him past the hedge into the courtyard. He approached a woman of twenty-four or -five, apparently the mistress of the house, who was setting out paper to dry.

When she heard from him the object of his visit, she hesitated. It was all too sudden. But when he showed her the letter, she seemed to be convinced. "I'm afraid I don't know anything about it," she said. "Won't you speak with the old one?" She called to a woman who was inside the house. It was Orito of the letter—the elder sister of Tsumura's mother.

Though rather taken aback by the intensity of his questions, she unraveled the threads of half-forgotten memories and replied, little by little, with her toothless mouth. Some of his questions she could not answer, having forgotten completely; sometimes her memory played tricks on her; she was hesitant to talk about some things; there were inconsistencies; she mumbled, and her breath whistled through her lips, making it difficult to understand her, and he sometimes could not get the gist no matter how often he asked her to repeat. Less than half of what she said was clear, and the rest he had to fill in with his imagination; but he learned enough to resolve the questions he had had about his mother for twenty years. The old woman said that she thought his mother had been sent to Osaka in the Keiō Period, or between 1865 and 1868, but she also said that she (who was now in her sixty-seventh year) had been thirteen or fourteen at the time, and his mother, eleven or twelve; and so of course it had to have been after the Meiji Restoration of 1868. That being the case, his mother had served in Shimmachi only two or three or, at the most, four years before marrying into the Tsumura family. He gathered from something Orito said that the Kombu family had indeed been in distressed circumstances; but being an old family that valued its reputation, they hid as best they could the fact that they had sent their daughter to such a place. Even after she had become the bride of a good family—and of course while she was still indentured—they rarely communicated with their daughter, thinking it an embarrassment both to her and to them. And the fact is that those who were indentured to the pleasure quarters, whether geisha, prostitutes, or teahouse girls, by custom severed all ties with their families as soon as the seals were affixed to the article of bondage. From that point on a family had no right to be involved with their daughter, no matter what became of her. The old woman did vaguely recall, however, that her mother had visited Osaka once or twice after the girl had been married into the Tsumura family: the mother had come back to tell in wonderment about her daughter, now mistress of an important family and living in luxury. There had also been a message urging Orito to come to Osaka, but she thought that she could hardly present her shabby figure in a place like that, nor did her sister ever visit Kuzu again, and so Orito never knew her as an adult. Presently her sister's husband died, and then her parents, whereupon all contact with the Tsumura family broke off completely. Orito always referred to her sister, Tsumura's mother, in a roundabout way, as "your dear mama." Perhaps she was simply being polite to

Tsumura, but it was also possible that she had forgotten her sister's name. When he asked about Oei, who went "every day into the mountains, where the snow is deep, to dig arrowroot," he learned that she had been the eldest daughter; Orito was the second, and the third was Tsumura's mother, Osumi. Oei had married into another family, while Orito's husband had been adopted and eventually became the head of the Kombu family. Both Oei and Orito's husband were now dead. The new head of the family was Orito's son Yoshimatsu, and it was Yoshimatsu's wife who had greeted Tsumura in the courtyard. While Orito's mother lived, she must have kept a few papers and letters relating to Osumi, but now, three generations later, hardly anything remained. After saying this, Orito seemed suddenly to remember something. She stood, opened the doors of the household Buddhist shrine, and brought out a photograph that was displayed among the memorial tablets. Tsumura remembered having seen it before. It was a small portrait photograph of his mother, taken shortly before her death. He had a copy of it in his album.

"Yes, yes . . . From your dear mama . . ." Orito seemed to have remembered something else. "Besides this photograph, there is a koto. Mother always treasured it, saying it was a memento of her daughter in Osaka. I haven't taken it out in a long time. I wonder what sort of condition it's in."

The koto was somewhere in the storeroom upstairs, she said. Tsumura waited for Yoshimatsu to come in from the fields and show it to him, and in the meantime ate lunch in the neighborhood. Returning to the house, he helped the young couple carry the unwieldy object, covered with a thick layer of dust, out to the verandah, where the light was good.

It was an incongruous heirloom for this house. Removing the faded oilcloth cover, they found an old, but splendid, lacquered koto, six feet long. Lacquer designs covered almost the entire instrument, except for the "shell" under the strings. The "shores" on either side were decorated with scenes of Sumiyoshi: on one side a shrine gate and an arched bridge were arranged in a pine forest; and the other side depicted a tall stone lantern, windblown pines, and waves on the beach. Countless plovers were in flight around the "sea," the "dragon horns," and the "four-six"; while near the "reed cloth," under the "oak leaf," the figure of an angel could be seen through five-color clouds. The underlying paulownia wood had darkened with age, so that the lacquer and paint struck the eye with an elegant, submerged light. Tsumura brushed the dust off the oilcloth and examined the design. The cloth appeared to be a *shioze* weave, heavy silk with prominent horizontal ribs. The upper part of the outer surface had a double-apricot-blossom crest in white on a red background, and on the lower part was a picture of a Chinese beauty seated in a tower and playing the koto. Two narrow, vertical tablets, inscribed with the lines of a Chinese couplet, hung on the columns of the tower:

> *She plays the twenty-five strings on a moonlit night.*
> *The geese flock north, unable to bear the pure, sad sound.*

The reverse side of the cover showed a formation of geese against the moon, beside which was a poem in Japanese:

> *I took them for*
> *A line of geese:*
> *Bridges on the koto*
> *Simulate the cloud paths.*

The double apricot was not, however, the crest of the Tsumura family. It may have been that of her foster family, the Urakado; or even that of the house in Shimmachi. Perhaps when she married into the Tsumura family, she no longer had any use for this relic of her days in the pleasure quarter, and sent it to her home in the country. It was also conceivable that there had been a girl of marriageable age in the family just then, for whom the old woman had accepted the instrument. On the other hand, Tsumura's mother may have kept it with her all those years in the Shimmachi house and left it to her family when she died. But Orito and the young couple knew nothing about it. They thought that there had once been a letter with the koto, but it was nowhere to be found now. They only remembered hearing that the koto had come from "the one we sent to Osaka."

THE PARTS OF A KOTO

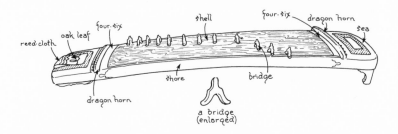

There was a small box for accessories, which contained the bridges and the plectra. The bridges were of dark hardwood, lacquered with a pine-bamboo-plum design. The plectra were worn down from long use. Moved by the thought that his mother had slipped them on her delicate fingers, Tsumura could not resist the urge to try one of the plectra on his little finger. The scene from his childhood, an elegant woman in an inner room performing "The Cry of the Fox" with her teacher, flitted before his eyes. The woman may not have been his mother, nor the koto this one; but probably his mother had played it many times as she sang the piece. He thought that he would like, if possible, to have the instrument reconditioned, and ask someone suitable to perform "The Cry of the Fox" on it for the anniversary of his mother's death.

The Inari shrine in the garden had been venerated for generations as the guardian deity of the family, and so the young couple was able to confirm what was in the letter on that subject. But there was no one in the family now who summoned foxes. As a child Yoshimatsu had heard rumors that his grandfather often did that sort of thing; but at some point "the white fox Myōbu-no-shin" had ceased to show himself, and now there was only an old foxhole in the shade of an oak chestnut behind the shrine. When Tsumura was taken to see it, he found a sacred rope stretched forlornly across the opening.

—The events of Tsumura's narrative took place the year of his grandmother's death, that is to say, two or three years before the day he told me the story as we sat on the rocks at Miyataki. The "relatives in Kuzu" whom he had mentioned in his letters to me were the old woman Orito and her family. Orito was, after all, Tsumura's maternal aunt, and her family was his mother's family. Accordingly, from that time on he had renewed the family connection between himself and his relatives. Not only that: he had also helped them financially, built a separate little house for his aunt, and enlarged the paper workshop. As a result, the Kombu family was able to pursue their little handicraft industry on a remarkably large scale.

6 ❧ SHIONOHA

"Then what is the purpose of this trip?" We were still resting on the rocks, forgetting the darkness that slowly gathered around us. Tsumura had reached a pause in his long tale. "Have you come to see your aunt?" I asked.

"Well, there is something I haven't told you about yet."

In the twilight we barely made out the foam on the rapids crashing against the rocks below us; but I could sense that Tsumura blushed slightly as he said this.

"When I stood outside the hedge at my aunt's house for the first time, there was a girl of seventeen or eighteen inside, making paper. Do you remember my saying that?"

"Yes."

"It turns out that she's the granddaughter of my other aunt—Aunt Oei, who died. She happened to be at the Kombu house that day, helping out."

Just as I thought, a note of embarrassment had crept into Tsumura's voice.

"As I said before, she's frankly a country girl, and not beautiful by any means. Working in the cold, and in the water as she does, her hands are unsightly and horribly chapped. But that line in the letter must have suggested something to me—'chapped and cracked and the tips of our fingers torn'—because, strangely, I took a liking to the girl the moment I saw her red hands in the water. And then, something about her features resembles my mother's face in the photographs. There's no denying that she's rather the maidservant type, because of the way she was brought up; but with a little polishing she might be more like my mother."

"I understand. Then she is your Hatsune drum?"

"Yes, that's right. . . . Well, what do you think? I'd like her to be my wife."

Her name was Owasa. Oei's daughter, Omoto, had married into a farming family named Ichida, who lived near Kashiwagi. Owasa was born there. Her family being hard pressed, though, she had gone to Gojō as a maidservant after completing primary school. She returned home at the age of seventeen, because the family was shorthanded, and helped with the farmwork. But in the winter, there being nothing to do, she was sent to the Kombu family to help with the papermaking. She would be there this year, too, but probably had not come yet. Tsumura wanted first to disclose his intentions to Aunt Orito and the young couple. Then, depending on the result, he would ask them to send for her immediately, or call on her himself.

"If all goes well, then, I'll be able to meet Owasa, too?"

"Yes. I invited you to come along on this trip so that you could meet her and tell me what you think. Our circumstances are so very different that I'm a little uneasy over whether we'd be happy if we married. I'm confident that it would be all right, but . . ."

At my urging, we got up from the rocks on which we had been sitting and hired a ricksha at Miyataki. By the time we arrived at the Kombu house in Kuzu, it was quite dark. As for my impressions of Orito and her family, the appearance of the house, and the papermaking facilities—it would be redundant to write about them here, and take up too much space. I will just mention several things that linger in my memory. Electricity had not yet come to the area, and so we spoke with the family seated around a large hearth under an oil lamp. It was the perfect mountain cottage. They used oak, both evergreen and deciduous, and mulberry wood in the hearth. Mulberry burned most slowly and gave off a gentle heat, they said, and they piled great quantities on the fire. I was astonished at the luxury of it, inconceivable in the city. The beams and ceiling above the hearth shone a lustrous black in the light of the crackling fire, as if they had just been painted with coal tar. Finally, the Kumano mackerel on our supper trays was delicious. Mackerel taken at the Kumano seashore were skewered on bamboo-grass leaves and brought over the mountains to be sold. During the five, six, or seven days on the way, they cured naturally in the air; and sometimes the dried fish were carried off by foxes—or so I was told.

The next morning, Tsumura and I decided that we would go about our activities separately for a while. Tsumura would take up the matter so important to him and persuade the Kombu family to help him arrange the marriage. So as not to be in the way, I would go on a five- or six-day trip to the source of the Yoshino River in search of material for my novel. Leaving Kuzu on the first day, I would pay my respects at the tomb of Prince Ogura, the son of Emperor Gokameyama, in Unogawa Village; then cross Gosha Pass to Kawakami Village and spend the night in Kashiwagi. On the second day I would cross Obagamine Pass and spend the night at Kawai in Kitayama Village. On the third day I would visit Ryūsen Temple in Kotochi, the site of the Heavenly King's palace, and Prince Kitayama's grave; then climb Ōdaigahara and spend a night in the mountains. On the fourth day I would pass Goshiki Hot Springs and explore Sannoko Canyon; then, if I could get through, I would go to see Hachiman Plain and Hidden Plain for myself, and ask for lodging in a woodcutter's hut, or come out to Shionoha for the night. On the fifth day I would return to Kashiwagi from Shionoha and, on the same day or the next, come back to Kuzu. This is the schedule that I devised after consulting the Kombu family on geography. Arranging to meet him later, I wished Tsumura success and started off. As I was leaving, Tsumura said that he might go to Owasa's house in Kashiwagi, and, explaining how to find it, asked me to stop there just in case, when I reached Kashiwagi on the way back.

My trip proceeded roughly according to schedule. I hear that nowadays even the rugged Obagamine Pass is traversed by buses, and one can go all the way to Kinomoto in Kii Province without walking. How much the world has changed since I made my trip. Favored by good weather, I was able to collect more material than I had expected and pushed on through the fourth day with little thought for hazards and difficulties; but I was undone by the entrance to Sannoko Canyon. Even before I reached it, people often said to me, "That's a hard place," or, "What! are you going to Sannoko?" and I thought I was prepared. Accordingly, I changed my schedule slightly on the fourth day and took a room at Goshiki Hot Springs. With a guide to help me, I started out the next morning. The road followed the Yoshino River downstream from its source on Mount Ōdaigahara. At a place called Ninomata, where another stream joined the river, the road divided in two, one fork leading straight to Shionoha, the other bending to the right and eventually penetrating Sannoko Canyon. The main road to Shionoha was unmistakably a road, but the right fork was a faint track through a dense cedar forest. To make matters worse, rain the night before had swollen the Ninomata River, washing away the log bridges or leaving them dangling precariously, so that I had to leap from rock to rock across the swirling torrent, and at times creep on all fours. In the upper reaches of the Ninomata River was an "Okutama River"; from there we crossed the

Jizō riverbed and finally reached the Sannoko River. The trail between the rivers threaded along the face of a precipitous cliff. In places the path was too narrow to accommodate both feet side by side, and in places it had fallen completely away. Logs or planks with crosspieces, lashed together in midair, spanned the gaps. In this manner the trail made its circuitous way, with many crooks and bends, along the cliffs. A mountaineer could have managed this trek before breakfast; but gymnastics were my downfall in middle school: the horizontal bar, ladder, and sidehorse always left me in tears. I was young at the time of the Yoshino trip, not so plump as I am now, and could easily walk twenty or twenty-five miles on flat ground; but here I had to proceed on my hands and knees, so that the issue was not the strength of my legs, but my overall physical condition. I am sure that I often went blue and red in the face. To tell the truth, I might have turned back at the Ninomata log bridge had I not been with a guide. I was ashamed in his presence, and to go back would have been as terrifying as to go forward; and so I advanced helplessly, my legs trembling. Consequently, though the autumn colors in the canyon were spectacular, I was so occupied with my footing that I lifted my eyes only when an occasional titmouse startled me by taking wing under my nose; and so, I am embarrassed to say, I lack the qualifications to describe the scenery in detail. My guide, however, was quite at ease. Holding in his mouth a cigarette made of shredded tobacco wrapped in a camellia leaf, he made his way effortlessly along the treacherous path. As he went, he identified for me the waterfalls and rocks in the canyon far below.

"That is the rock called Gozenmōsu," he said at one point; then, a little further on: "That is the rock called

Berobedo." With my frightened glances at the canyon
floor, I could not be sure which was Berobedo and which
Gozenmōsu, but my guide told me that there had to be
rocks by these names in a canyon formerly occupied by the
King. Four or five years before, an important person from
Tokyo—a scholar, perhaps, or a professor, or a government
official, in any case an eminent person—had come to see the
canyon. "Is there a rock here called Gozenmōsu?" he asked,
to which my guide responded, "Aye, sir, there is," and indicated a certain rock. "Then is there a rock called Berobedo?" "Aye, sir, there is," he replied, pointing to another
rock. "Well, well. In that case the Heavenly King was here,
without any question," and he returned to Tokyo very
much impressed. Such is the story my guide told, but he did
not know the origin of these peculiar names.

He was familiar with various other legends as well. The
pursuers from the capital, not knowing where the Heavenly
King was living, searched from mountain to mountain. One
day, happening upon this canyon, they saw gold flowing
toward them in the river, and traced the flow of gold
upstream until they found the palace. Another story was
that after he moved to the Kitayama Palace, the King went
every morning to wash his face in the Kitayama River,
which flowed before the palace. He was always accompanied by two doubles, so that no one could tell which
was the real King. The pursuers asked an old village woman
who chanced to come by. She told them, "That one, whose
breath is white, is the King." Thanks to her, the pursuers
were able to attack and take the King's head; but for generations thereafter, the old woman's descendants were born
crippled.

At about one o'clock in the afternoon I arrived at a hut
on Hachiman Plain, where I opened my lunch and recorded

these legends in my notebook. It was another seven miles to Hidden Plain and back, but the path was easier than the one I had taken in the morning. Even so, however much the Southern courtiers wanted to escape notice, the head of this valley was just too inaccessible. Surely Prince Kitayama's poem was not composed at this place.

> *Fleeing here I settle*
> *In the mountain depths and dwell*
> *Behind a brushwood door—*
> *My heart is one with the moon.*

In short, Sannoko may be the site of legends, but not of history. That night, my guide and I stayed in a mountain man's house at Hachiman Plain and were treated to a supper of rabbit meat. The next day we took the same path back to Ninomata, where I parted company with my guide and went alone to Shionoha. I had heard that it was only two and a half miles from here to Kashiwagi, but there were hot springs at the edge of the river, and so I went to bathe. A suspension bridge spanned the Yoshino River where it widened with the added flow of the Ninomata. Crossing, I found the springs on the riverbank directly under the bridge. But when I tested the water with my hand, it was no hotter than water warmed by the sun. Farm women were busily washing radishes in it.

"You can only bathe here in the summer. This time of year, we put the water in that tub over there, and heat it." The women pointed to a tub lying on the riverbank. Just as I turned to look, someone called to me from the suspension bridge above.

"Hello!"

It was Tsumura, crossing the bridge toward me with a girl, no doubt Owasa, behind him. The bridge swayed slightly under their weight and the sound of their wooden sandals echoed in the valley.

I never wrote the historical novel I had planned; there was a bit more material than I could handle. But of course Owasa, whom I saw on the bridge that day, is now Tsumura's wife. The trip was more fruitful for Tsumura than for me.

Japanese foxes have certain magical powers. For one thing, they can assume the form of any person or object, and frequently use this ability to make mischief with humans. In Tanizaki's play *White Fox Hot Springs*, a young farmer is bewitched by a fox that has taken the form of a beautiful foreign woman. He dies; but another Tanizaki victim of fox-mischief is more fortunate. In "A Fox Bewitches a Lacquer-Gatherer in the Province of Kii," a tale published with *Arrowroot* in 1932, the woodsman of the title manages to escape unharmed.

There are also benevolent foxes. The most famous example is the fox-mother in the kabuki play *Arrowroot Leaves:* a devoted wife and mother, she parts with her human family only when her disguise is exposed. Another appealing fox is Genkurō, who assumes the form of Yoshitsune's faithful retainer Tadanobu in *Yoshitsune and the Thousand Cherry Trees*, so that he can be near the drum on which his parent's skin is stretched.

Some people are under the special protection of foxes, as Tsumura's grandparents seem to be. More generally, foxes are believed to be messengers of Inari, the Harvest God and guardian of farmers and sword-makers. Fox statues are invariably to be found at the entrance to an Inari shrine.

Foxes are so partial to tempura and fried tofu that they can be summoned by setting out these delicacies. As we learn in *Arrowroot*, they also have a weakness for dried fish.

A . H . C .

A NOTE ABOUT THE AUTHOR

Junichirō Tanizaki was born in 1886 in Tokyo, where his family owned a printing establishment. He studied Japanese literature at Tokyo Imperial University, and his first published work, a one-act play, appeared in 1909 in a literary magazine he helped to found.

Tanizaki lived in the cosmopolitan Tokyo area until the earthquake of 1923, when he moved to the gentler and more cultivated Kyoto-Osaka region, the scene of his great novel *The Makioka Sisters* (1943–48). There he became absorbed in the Japanese past, and abandoned his superficial westernization. His most important novels were written after 1923; among them are *A Fool's Love* (1924), *Some Prefer Nettles* (1928), *Manji* (1930), *Ashikari* (1932), *A Portrait of Shunkin* (1933), modern versions of *The Tale of Genji* (1941, 1954, and 1965), *The Makioka Sisters, Captain Shigemoto's Mother* (1949), *The Key* (1956), and *Diary of a Mad Old Man* (1965). By 1930 he had gained such renown that an edition of his "Complete Works" was published. He received the Imperial Prize in Literature in 1949 and died in 1965.

A NOTE ABOUT THE TRANSLATOR

Anthony H. Chambers took his doctorate in Japanese literature at the University of Michigan in 1974. He is Associate Professor of Asian Languages and Literatures at Wesleyan University.

A NOTE ON THE TYPE

The text of this book was set on the Linotype in Janson, a recutting made directly from type cast from matrices long thought to have been made by the Dutchman Anton Janson, who was a practicing type founder in Leipzig during the years 1668–87. However, it has been conclusively demonstrated that these types are actually the work of Nicholas Kis (1650–1702), a Hungarian, who most probably learned his trade from the master Dutch type founder Dirk Voskens. The type is an excellent example of the influential and sturdy Dutch types that prevailed in England up to the time William Caslon developed his own incomparable designs from them.

The book was composed by The Maryland Linotype Composition Company, Baltimore, Maryland. It was printed and bound by R. R. Donnelley & Company, Harrisonburg, Virginia.

Typography and binding design
by Dorothy Schmiderer